Z Day is Here

a journal of the zombie apocalypse

By
Rob Fox

A "Library of the Living Dead" Book
Published by arrangement with the author.

"Z Day is Here"
By Rob Fox
Copyright 2009 Rob Fox All Rights Reserved

ISBN10 - 1448603072
ISBN13 - 9781448603077

Without limiting the rights under copyright reserved above, no part of this publication may be reproduced, stored, or introduced into a retrieval system, or transmitted in any form, or by any means (electronic, mechanical, photocopying, recording, or otherwise) without the prior written permission of both the copyright owner and "Library of the Living Dead Press", except in the case of brief quotations embodied in critical articles and reviews.

This book is a work of fiction. People, places, events, and situation are the product of the author's imagination. Any resemblance to actual persons, living, dead or undead, or historical events, is purely coincidence.

Dedication

To my Grandparents for listening to my stories by the campfire and teaching me it is okay to have an imagination.

This book would not be possible without the love and support from many people. There are too many friends and not enough room to list everyone that supported me through this process. My thanks to all of you are within the pages of this book.

I would like to give a very special Thanks to my wonderful wife Darcy, who pushed me to finish the blog/book and who put up with the many evenings of stress and sleepless nights while I was writing it. I love you.

I would also like to thank everyone who read the blog and continually asked "what happens next?" Without the constant nagging, I would have stopped writing long ago.

Finally, yes, Denna, you are "Mego".

Enjoy

A Note From Dr. Pus

Searches on the internet can find you weird and wonderful things. Point in fact, "Z Day is Here". Quite a while ago I was looking for something new to add to the "Library of the Living Dead Podcast" and typed in "zombie", hit the search and up popped a plethora of zombie sites, mine included. But there, right there, was something about a blog concerning the zompocalypse. I clicked on the link, read the writers name ….. never heard of him before. I certainly have now.

What I found was a wonderful journal (if I may be so bold as to say the zombie apocalypse is wonderful) by Rob Fox. I contacted him immediately to ask if I could present the 101 day journal on the podcast. It was an instant hit with the Good Librarians.

When I decided to start publishing zombie novels I thought immediately about publishing Rob's "Z Day is Here" in dead tree format. Rob diligently rewrote the entire journal, Editor Supreme Becca did the tweaking and Dan Galli let his talents be used for the cover.

That Good Librarian is what you now hold in your hands. A fantastic tale of a man surrounded by a world being destroyed by the undead horde.

Welcome to the Zompocalypse,

Doc

Day 1

    Scared as hell....that's about the only way to describe how I'm feeling. It just happened so fast. Five days ago the news came in that a little boy - Shawn Crockett I think was his name - was brutally attacked while traveling in South America with his mother. As the news reported, Shawn was kidnapped, beaten, and left for dead outside of some Mayan ruins. Some locals found him barely breathing and covered in bite marks. It was a circus. Every time I turned on the TV, that damn kid's face kept popping up...kind of made me sick. I just got tired of hearing about him. The next day news stories came in that Little Shawn Crockett passed away. The world mourned. The press blamed it on some strange rabies strain. It wasn't until the press conference that the world went from crying over little Shawn to hating and fearing him. While the doctors were announcing the actual news of his death, via a live feed, a single scream could be heard from inside the hospital. I will never forget that scream. Over the PA systems and hounding reporters, you could hear a screech of horror and pain. I was sitting on my couch trying to find something - ANYTHING on TV other than that crap....but that scream. Apparently, the guy doing the autopsy was attacked by a now undead Shawn Crockett.

    Rabies....that's what they kept saying...stay calm...contamination...quarantine...the next few days, that's all we heard. Then, no news...or scattered rumors here and there..... Death everywhere....or undead everywhere. I am hidden at my job… a nice stronghold of a building…. nothing can get in here.

That leads us up to today August 28th, 2007. I am writing this blog for the history books. So maybe one day when we are all long gone, the grandchildren of the survivors can know what happened. Thank God the internet is still up. I will blog on here as much as I can, to update the world on the status of the uprising.

For now, I have to go scavenge food from the break room...I hear something on the other side of the door though...shit! I'm starving… I should have stayed at home. God I hope my fiancé's still alive. I'll try to get her as soon as I can. Right now all I can think about is food…. that must be how these undead bastards feel.

Ok, it's quiet out there...wish me luck.

Day 2

Well, as you can see from this entry, I made it! When I walked out the door....yeah, like I just walked right out the door! More like crawled out the door like a wounded puppy scurrying away from his attacker. So anyway, I got out of the "safe" area and slowly made my way down the hall...nothing! silence! Thank God! As I turned the corner I could just barely make out the body of my manager. Amanda was her name. She was just lying there on the ground, a huge chunk missing from her face. My thoughts went to her kids. She had two really cute kids...a boy and a girl, I think. Now all I could think about was her kids being without their mom. Hell, her kids were probably like those freaks out there....eating the brains of their father! I knew I hated kids for a reason....creepy little bastards.

As I watched my manager laying on the ground in front of me....fresh blood trickling down her thin cheek, looking so peaceful, I heard a noise behind me. I jumped and quickly spun around...nothing there....must have been the wind I thought. I turned back to make my way to the break room. Amanda was gone!! A pool of blood where she was last seen 5 seconds ago laying dead. How could I have been so stupid!!

To my left, I saw her coming at me, that slack jaw begging to taste my flesh. I didn't think, I just dove into the closest office. Begging God to help me, I slipped and fell onto the floor. So stupid......she was still coming after me. Again, I didn't think, I just reacted. I grabbed the closest "blunt object" I could find. A fish bowl! I grabbed a fucking fish bowl and she pounced on me. I could smell the stink of her breath as her lips brushed my neck. I couldn't scream; all I could do was swing the fish bowl. Bang! It smashed right across her face. Now, I have hit people in the face before, but never this hard and never with a fish bowl....poor fish, it never had a chance. I staggered up, looked down at Amanda laying on the ground, a fresh chunk of skull had been taken out of her head. I could see the side of her brain and a piece of fish sticking out the side of her skull. She moved! I grabbed a ball point pen from the desk and shoved it in the gash and stirred her brains into mush like oatmeal. She never moved again.

I made my way to the break room. It was like being in heaven! I packed my pockets full of the sweet junk food that I had stayed away from for so long. Three Cokes in my right hand, and now a knife I found in the drawer, in my left hand. I hiked my way back to the "safe room". When I got inside, I ....

Wait! I hear something in here...

Day 3

Well, my safe room is no longer safe. I've got to be more careful. I propped the door open to the room yesterday while I was gone to get food and three of the undead bastards got in. While I was typing the entry for yesterday, I heard a noise behind me....it's the noise they all make; kind of a low growl. It's like they are angry at the living for not being one of them.

I turned around just in time to see two of the three trying to make my head their next meal. I jumped so far back I knocked over the computer. Thank God they are slow movers...they kind of hobble around, shambling their feet one after the other, like they have nowhere to go. But in this case, they had somewhere to go...straight to the buffet that is me! I made my way out of the room and down the hall where I pass by a still dead Amanda laying in the same spot where I left her....head still gashed open, fish still impaled on the piece of scalp.

I looked away from the room just in time to see four more of them standing directly in my path. My only choice was to run outside. The open was the last place I wanted to be. I got to the door...no zombies around. My car was sitting there in the parking lot, so inviting. I took off out the door, running at full speed towards the car, opened the door, sat down, closed the door and realized that I LEFT MY FUCKING KEYS INSIDE THE OFFICE!

BAM! Five zombies suddenly surround the car; banging on the windows, that low growl getting louder and louder. It must be a signal to the others because eight more zombies surrounded the car, pounding on the windows, trying desperately to get in. I gave up, no need to fight; one or two maybe, but not 13 with more coming. My time was over...I began to wonder what it would feel like to be one of them...what was it like to eat flesh. Would they even make me one of them? I mean, what if they just destroyed my body so badly that I couldn't come back?

I looked out the window one last time as if to say good bye to the world when I see an angel. She was beautiful, with long blond hair, very slender, yet athletic. By the terror on her face, as well as the blood coming from her arms and side, I could tell she had been bitten...hell, she had been half eaten. I'm not sure how she had survived this long with all that blood loss, but I knew is she was as good as dead already. Once the zombies got a whiff of her fresh blood, they pounced on her like lions on a downed wildebeest. She went down within seconds. I remember watching National Geographic as a kid and more recently, Discovery channel, watching some tigers in Africa take down a wounded elephant, then eat it as it struggled to survive. I was now watching this again, though not in Africa, and not with tigers and elephants....this time with a live human girl and zombies. They ripped the flesh from her bones without even trying.

I saw my opening! I opened the door and took off running. I didn't looked back and didn't slow down. I made my way to an old industrial building about 3 miles from my work. The whole way, I saw zombie after zombie; people screaming and running, begging for help, cars speeding by trying anything they could do to get away. I saw an occasional person peeking out of their house window with gun in hand. They would just shake their heads "no", to tell me to stay away or else. I don't blame them at all, I would do the same. I'm not in a very safe place, but I have no choice. I am exhausted and hungry.

I've got to make my way toward my house ... toward my love. God I pray she is still alive. Ok, I have to rest for awhile and try to get some sleep, if I can.

Day 4

Sleep! Ahhh glorious sleep. I haven't slept this good in days...and with a full belly!

Yesterday while I was at the industrial building, I was walking around the perimeter, securing the doors and blocking the windows (Kind of felt a little like Ann Frank must have; a prisoner in my own land) when I saw a quick flash in a nearby door way. Christ! There were more in here I thought! Looking around, I found a nice big metal pipe; if a fish bowl would knock someone down; this would surely bash their skull in with little force. I readied myself, preparing for the impending attack. My stance - just like a baseball player. Ready, waiting for the pitch...but this wasn't a baseball; this was a human head...If you can even call it human anymore. I heard it coming closer to me, then more footsteps. Great, I thought, I was going to have to battle more than just one. I saw another flash! One just to my right! My military training taught me to go for the closest threat, so I spun around, pulled the pipe back, ready to attack...Bam! I was tackled! Something came out of nowhere, got me from behind. How, how could it have moved so quickly, so silently??

It wasn't a zombie. In fact, none of them in the building were. I had stumbled onto a compound of 4 people. This group had done what I had; found a safe location to stay for a while.

First there was Reggie; he is the one that tackled me. Then there was Eliza and her husband Mike, who ran a local dog kennel, and finally there was Darrell, who I found out later ran a local video game shop. Once the formalities were out of the way, we sat around and talked. We talked about the zombies (of course) and about what we had seen and experienced so far. We all had similar stories, as well as people we wanted to go home to.

Reggie was an ex-football star (hence the tackle), who had injured his shoulder during his first pro game. He had been on his way to meet his girlfriend in South Carolina, when the SUV he was traveling in was struck by a tractor trailer. Apparently the tractor trailer swerved to miss a group of people "just standing in the road"; I am sure they were probably zombies. That's where Mike and Eliza came in. They were in a car a few vehicles behind Reggie, on their way to a dog grooming convention, when they saw a truck slam into the side of the SUV. The tractor kept going, so Mike decided to stop and see if he could help. While he was helping, he was attacked by one of the zombies. He got bit on his left bicep. He knows he is as good as dead, but wants to spend as much time with his wife as he can before his "change".

    Darrell was the first to find the warehouse. He had been staying here for a few days now. He was on his way to his parent's house for the weekend, when all hell broke loose. I guess running a video game store has its advantages, because he seemed to know a lot about killing zombies. He said his knowledge came from the video games. *And they said video games were the downfall of us all!*
    Last night was a good night. I bet it will probably be the last good night we will have for a while. Mike woke up this morning with a very high fever. His arm looks like it has taken on a life of its own. It has begun twitching for no reason and the wound looks like month old ground beef. He's not going to make it much longer. Darrell has already volunteered to "bash his face in" the second he changes....though I believe he would do it before Mike even changed. Eliza is in denial., poor girl. I don't know how she will react when all this goes down, which based on how quickly Mike is changing, could be within the next few hours.

Day 5

It has hit the fan! Don't have much time to write about it. All I can say is I am alone again, injured, and looking for a new safe house. Before you all start getting worried, No! It is not a zombie bite. I will go into greater details in the morning. I am not feeling real good right now...must be the loss of blood.

Day 6

The pain! I think my ankle is broken. The pain had me knocked out for hours. My laptop got a good charge though!

SO where do I begin...how can I even come close to explaining what happened. The words that my fingers are about to type will never come close to the horrors that befell me a couple of days ago. But I should...No! I have to try to explain what happened; maybe for my own sanity or maybe out of respect for the others, or just to take my mind off the pain.

Let me take you back to yesterday morning. We were all still getting to know each other. Telling stories of our families, our work, and rumors we had heard about what was going on. Darrell had a wife and two daughters - all three are now dead. Reggie had a long time girlfriend and a little boy - their status was unknown. Eliza had Mike - Mike was getting worse by the second. I had Darcy, my love, my fiancé – her status regretfully, is unknown.

As we talked throughout the day we were at peace for the first time in days. It was as if we were at a high school reunion, playing catch up with all our old friends. Zombies, what zombies? Zombies don't exist. But they do, and we were not long time friends just catching up. We were the survivors of a terrible tsunami of the living dead coming to wash away all of mankind. Every time we looked at Mike we were reminded of this.

Sometime late in the afternoon, Mike excused himself to go check on the barricades. Darrell volunteered to go with him while Reggie, Eliza and I stayed behind to clean up our mess - zombie attack or not, Eliza would not have a messy shelter!
I'm not sure what I heard first, the gun shot, or the scream...both sounds will forever haunt me the rest of my life.....no matter how short it may be.

We all went running toward the noise and as we turned the corner, we saw Darrell with his snub nose revolver still smoking, shaking in his right hand. Mike was laying in the fetal position on the ground by the front door. A look of shock and disbelief forever painted on his face. A very large hole now replaced his eyebrow. All I could think to say was "What the hell have you done?"

Darrell turned to look at us. "He was about to change...he was about to change I...." He dropped the gun and ran for the front door. Pulling away the barricades, he could only apologize and repeat "He was changing". Reggie went for one of his signature tackling moves, doing whatever he could do to keep Darrell from opening the door. Five steps away. Hell, maybe even closer, a single gunshot rang out from behind me. Darrell crashed through the front door. Maybe crashed isn't the proper word to use. I guess I should say he flew through the door. That's what happens when a bullet tears through your back and explodes out your chest.

I turned to see Eliza holding the pistol. A look of pure hatred spread across her face. I flinched at what I had just witnessed. I couldn't take my eyes off sweet little Eliza, whose husband had just been taken away from her; who in a matter of seconds had become a killer. No, she had become an executioner.

I stared too long and before I knew it, half a dozen zombies had entered the room. Within another 30 seconds the room was full of the undead. "RUN!" Reggie snapped me from my trance with a yell and a tug on my shirt. I ran for the window with Reggie directly in front of me. Eliza ran as well, however, she ran straight into a pack of zombies. Now, I will never know for sure, but I would almost swear I heard her yell "Wait for me Mikey. I'll see you soon". She was pulled into four pieces before I could even make it to the window. She didn't scream in pain or cry out in fear. She went to be with her husband whom she loved.

Reggie burst through the window on a mission. He was not going to be the next meal. I was right behind him. On the ledge of the window, we looked down. Shit! We were on the third floor! We had to choose. Be eaten alive or break our necks jumping. I chose to take my chances with the demons behind me. Surely I could get around them, they moved really slow; I thought the odds were better going around them. Reggie chose to jump and take me with him. As he hurled himself out the window, he grabbed my shirt. I had no choice but to follow.

When we hit, I heard the crunch. The crunch of my ankle cracking against the edge of the dumpster Reggie was aiming for. He was off his mark, by, pardon the pun, a foot. I had no time to think about the pain before I was surrounded by three zombies. The stench of their rotting flesh nearly chocked me. I was done for, there was no way I could get up in time and no way could I run. WACK! The sound the 2x4 made as it smashed across the left cheek of the nearest zombie was music to my ears. Reggie grinned as he swung the 2x4 twice more, offing the remaining two surrounding me. He was so pleased with himself that he didn't notice the one behind him. His grin quickly turned to pain as the undead former Burger King employee chomped down on my savior's neck. Blood flew in all directions as he fell to the ground.

I jumped to my feet and hobbled off as fast as I could. Pain no longer an option. Just getting to safety is all I could think about. Just about three miles later, my ankle was swollen to the size of a grapefruit and the color of a ripe plum. I ducked into a really nice multi-million dollar home that appeared to be vacant. I barricaded the doors and tried to cover the windows as best I could throughout the house. I found the master bathroom, locked myself in and passed out for a few hours. I woke long enough to bandage up my scrapes and wrap my ankle, before I passed out from the pain again.

The house is blessedly quiet. I will check it out a little more tomorrow. As for me tonight, I am going to take a shower and sleep more.

Good night Eliza, Mike, Darrell, and Reggie. May God tuck you away into his loving arms. You will all be missed.

Day 7

The swelling has gone down quite a bit since last night. I soaked my ankle in cold water for most of the night and most of today. There hasn't been any action today - thank God. I wandered through the house today, looking through drawers and cabinets. You really learn about a family when you have full access to their personal belongings. It appears this place was owned by a Bill and Becky Allen. They had two children, both girls. Looks like a new born and a pre-teen. Judging by the amount of blood I found in the kitchen area and in the swimming pool, I doubt any of them survived the first wave of flesh eaters. Bill was a doctor and from what I can tell, a heart surgeon. Since it appeared to be a newborn baby in one of the photos in the living room, I am guessing Becky was at home with the kids most of the time. Wild scenarios danced through my head about how the family must have fought off the killers, desperately struggling to save their children from the undead savages. Bill would have taken out two of them while Becky screamed and cried in the corner; sheltering her new baby...pleading with the monsters as they violently ripped the squalling child from her arms. What horror it must have been watching their pre-teen baby girl devoured before their eyes, knowing there is nothing they could do. Would Bill and Becky have finally given up their lives so they could be together as a family again? Or would they have fought until their final breath in order to survive? Either way, I believe in the end, these high-class millionaires were turned into brain eating morons. Life is cruel. The undead are even crueler.

I swear I will not allow myself to become one of them....I can't. My God, what if I became a zombie and found my love Darcy hiding in a corner...would I eat her? Could I? What if she is a zombie already? Could I bash her skull in? Should I even attempt to find her?
I think I am going crazy. Everyone around me is dead or undead. The living are going insane...like me. Can I continue to survive like this? Do I want to survive like this? The doctor has pills in his medicine cabinet. I could take just a hand full and this would be all over. I wouldn't have to worry about the zombies or the pain in my ankle. I wouldn't have to worry about anything anymore…I …wait, someone is here!

It's Dr. Allen...

Day 8

Death is all around me. Two weeks ago I was nothing more than a networking engineer, now I am a harbinger of death. I have killed zombies and now I have killed a living breathing human.

I heard a loud bang and someone whistling some old song that I can vaguely remember my grand- father whistling when I was a child. He was walking through the house as if he had not a care in the world. He walked right into the kitchen, not even glancing at the blood splattered floor, walls, and cabinets. He opened the refrigerator door, got out some lunchmeat, cheese, mayo and bread, and then sat down to make himself a sandwich! I sat in the hall closet watching this man eat a sandwich while being surrounded by the blood of his family. I watched him as he finished his sandwich, cleaned off his face, and then walked out the back door and made his way to the tool shed in the back yard.

When he reemerged from the shed, I was in complete disbelief! He walked out with his wife....only she wasn't the same as she was in the pictures hung so neatly on the wall. She was now one of the undead! She was missing her arms and most of her midsection. I couldn't be sure, but I could swear I saw her spine through what was once her stomach. He had her on a leash, with a ball gag in her mouth.
He brought her inside, chained her to the refrigerator, and pulled his chair up next to her. I could just barely make out what he was saying, but from what I could hear, the conversation (although one sided), went something like..."Becky?...Becky?" She did not respond. "Now Becky, I told you when I call your name, you better listen to me!" "I hate seeing you suffer like this". She did not respond. "Well honey, I took care of the girls, so now it's j

just you and me. I really hated to do it, but they can't live in a world like this. They begged me not to do it, but I had no choice. They are better off this way."

When I heard this, I recoiled in horror. I could not listen to this any longer.

I crept out of the closet, made my way to the "good" doctor's office. Looking around, I found a baseball bat signed by Chipper Jones and hanging in a nice glass case on the wall. I grabbed the bat and headed to the kitchen. He was gone!

"Who the Hell are you?" I heard this as he came up behind me. I spun around and smacked him in the head with the bat, as hard as I could. I didn't' ask questions, I didn't allow him to explain. I just simply hit him. He hit the ground, dropping a plastic bag full of something that appeared to be chunks of flesh - no doubt one of his children.

He was not moving and just barely breathing. I hit him again, removing a good portion of his scalp this time. I struck him again, this time he stopped breathing all together.

I searched his body and found car keys!

I then walked into the kitchen and allowed Becky to follow her husband.

I glanced out-side to see a brand new shiny SUV sitting in the driveway. I will leave this cursed house tonight! Darcy, if you are still alive, I am coming for you.

Day 9

Fate or luck? After a week of pure hell, it looks like things are beginning looking a little better. So yesterday I got in the SUV to drive home; it was the first time in a vehicle since all this started. God it was great to be driving again. The roads were in bad shape though. Cars parked in the middle of the road, or in someone's house. There were cars with busted out windows - no doubt the owners dragged out and eaten alive. I also passed by hordes of zombies. The numbers have gotten much larger since the first wave of them. They are all ages and all sizes. They are indiscriminate on who they choose to devour. There were toddlers walking - or limping down the road. Instead of a teddy bear hanging from their tiny hands, they were carrying a severed hand or foot. There were elderly men and women, and there were supermodels and bums. I saw a man in a business suite fighting with a woman in a KFC uniform over the body of what appeared to be a middle aged man.

I was getting closer to my house. I'm still quite a few

miles away, but closer than I was this time the day before. The interstates were completely shut down, so I was forced to take back roads.

I pass neighborhoods that were barricaded, armed gunmen keeping a close watch; it's as if I am living in a war zone. How has this happened? How long can we keep this up? The power has to go off at some point. The phones are all down and cell phones are useless. Nothing on the radio except for the same old warning, "stay in your houses, help is on the way" or "make your way to the nearest fallout shelter."; no doubt a recording. Where is the military during all this? We will soon be forced back to the middle ages. This destruction after only a week! What will it look like after a month or a year?

While driving, my mind wandered to far off places and times long past. I never noticed the gas light flashing red; warning me that I will soon be walking. I finally noticed it about two seconds before the car stalled. It would not crank back up. Well, it was good while it lasted. I grab my bat and the few supplies I had packed before I left the house and hit the ground running. After less than a mile, my ankle had swollen back to the size of a grapefruit. To my left was a group of the undead. They had not spotted me yet. It was only a matter of time until they smelled my living organs.

I felt a cold rush of air against my neck as two small

hands covered my mouth. As I turned, I could see a kid; couldn't be a day over 15. He dropped his hands from my face and was motioning me to follow but to be quiet. I followed, not knowing what I was getting into, just knowing I had no choice. The boy led me back to a large house...more like an encampment...or a fortress. There was a large brick wall surrounding the house, with barb wire around the top. We came to a large metal door. Metal spikes sticking out of the middle of it, waiting to impale anyone stupid enough to come close. This reminded me of the last Mad Max movie. The boy whistled and the metal door creaked open very slightly, just enough for us to get inside, then instantly closed behind us. Once inside, we were surrounded by a group of teenagers and a woman who appeared to be in her mid to late 30's. Her name was Deanna. The boy who saved me was named Cole. He was her son. The others were friends of his who were spending the night when the shit hit the fan. They found this old house with the large wall around it, and made it their own. Not much has happened since I got here. I did sleep pretty good last night and Deanna made some good soup, so I have a full stomach again. I am not sure how long I will stay here, but here is safer than out there. They do patrols every hour and monitor the perimeter constantly. I feel safe here. They are all very optimistic of the future which is exactly what I need right now.

    Has fate finally come to my rescue, or is it just luck? Either way, I will enjoy it as long as I can.

Day 10

The moaning! The undead constantly bang on the outside walls....and the constant moaning! All night and all day today so far all I hear is the low painful moaning. They never shut up. I hate them; I hate them all. Ok, I've got to get a grip; I have to calm down. I couldn't sleep because of the noise; between the moaning of those bastards and the constant whining of the teenagers. I can't help but laugh, kind of feels like I'm at a *My Chemical Romance* concert. When the outbreak started, they were spending the night with that Cole kid; celebrating his birthday; not a care in the world. Then all hell broke loose. Together as a group they made their way from neighborhood to neighborhood until they found this place. They have been lucky so far; Deanna has kept them from seeing a lot of the horrors going on around them. They know what is going on, but they have not seen what I have. They haven't had to kill their supervisor or watch people get mauled right before their eyes. They haven't been pulled out of a window, nor have they had to beat a man to death. How can I live with myself? He was a living breathing human; he was one of us. Who made me judge, jury, and executioner??

I woke up this morning after about an hour of sleep, to moaning and crying. When I walked out of the room I was "issued", it was bright outside. Most of the kids were huddled up, discussing the plan for the day with Deanna. Off to the side there were two kids...twins, holding each other and crying while other children tried to comfort them. That's when I noticed something that will forever haunt me for the rest of my life...

Propped up against a wall, blood smeared and sweaty was a young girl, holding a new born. I knew these children. I have seen them before. I spent the past few nights in their house. It was Dr. Allen's children! He had not killed his children as I had thought. This was his way of "taking care of the kids" He had found this place; a safe place for his children and went back to be with his wife; he loved his children so much he could not stand losing them as well.

What have I done? The zombies have taken these girls mother and I have robbed them of their father...I am evil. But I didn't know. How could I have known? I am a murderer. I am no better than those flesh eaters on the outside of the walls.

I have to leave this place...I don't deserve to live. I am sorry Darcy...if your still alive, I love you..

I am going out the gates...

Day 11

Rain.

Rain has a way of washing away the old and dirty and making it look nice and clean. Special people also have that ability.

Yesterday I was all set to walk out the front gates and end my miserable life. I would let the undead do their worst to me, because I felt I deserved it. I was set and ready. I had made piece with God. I reached the front gate, had my hand on the latch that would deliver me to certain death, when it started raining. Not just a slight rain, a monsoon came from the sky. I paused just long enough for Deanna to see me. She came running out into the rain, grabbing me by the arm and began pulling me back to the house. I stopped her just short of the front porch. Right there standing in the pouring down rain, I broke down. I was sobbing and confessing my sins to a complete stranger. She never tried to stop me; not that she could. I had things I had to say to someone. I told her of all I had done and what I was planning. She just looked at me, frowned and hugged me. There in the pouring down rain, we cried together. The rain has a way of washing away the old and dirty and making it look nice and clean again.

We walked back to the house hand in hand. As we reached the front porch, someone screamed right outside the outer wall. We all ran to the front gate, weapons in hand and ready to strike. As we pulled open the gate, One of the kids came running in, covered in blood and very pale. We slammed the gate shut as five zombies acceded on us. One of the ghouls got his arm through just as we were slamming it shut. The arm was severed just below the elbow; no one stopped to look at it though. No one even watched it as it crawled across the ground, aimlessly wandering around looking for its owner, or its next victim. Instead, we all stared in disbelief as one of our own stood before us in the rain with a fresh chunk of flesh taken out of his arm. He was infected. He was 14 years old. He was Cole's best friend.

How long now? How long before we must kill this young boy?

This time, I curse the rain.

Day 12

Stupid kids. A rumor went around about how we were going to kill the kid that got bit. Cole decided he couldn't let his friend die, so they both ran off. I am gathering some supplies to go out looking for them....stupid kids...I'm only doing this because Deanna has threatened to go out herself. She saved my life, now I have to save hers. I have to get to them before the zombies do or before Cole's little friend turns into one. Either way, I am sure I will have good stories when I get back - if I get back. Wish me luck.

Day 13

    I have been out and about all night and all day today and have yet to find Cole or his soon-to-be zombie friend. Damn teenagers, they always think they are right. Why the hell am I even out here? I could just say forget that stupid kid, and head home. But what kind of person would that make me? I hate my conscience. I have been put through Hell the past few hours and for what? Some kid that will either be dead or ungrateful that I am there to save him....me saving someone...yeah, I'm a regular Superman.

    So yesterday getting out of the gate was no easy task. I had my trusty bat...the same bat I used to kill an innocent man with, and some food and water. I opened the gate slightly. Only two zombies were standing at the front. They were walking directly into the wall, like a blind dog after moving the furniture around in the house. They must have been blind before their "change". I stepped out into the still wet sidewalk. The gate slammed shut. Before I could even think, both blind zombies smelled their next meal. They both turned toward me with their mouths hanging open, fresh blood and meat hanging from their incisors. I waited for them to get close to me. With one strong swing, the bat struck them both in the head. The bat made contact with the first one, his head slammed into the second ones. They both hit the ground. Both still very much alive or undead, however you wish to call it. I took out all my anger on both of them. I bashed their skulls into the ground as if I were playing the Whack-A-Mole game I used to play at Chuckee Cheese, only this time, I didn't win any tickets. Covered in zombie blood and exhausted, I made my way into the woods surrounding the complex. I decided to keep to the shadows and avoid fights and confrontations as much as possible.

    I think humans are losing this war. The undead were everywhere. Maybe it was the zombie blood covering up my stench, because there were many times I would pass by a group of them and they would not even glance at me. I'll have to remember that. I'm not sure as to why the blood doesn't change me; maybe it has something to do with the blood hitting the air. Maybe whatever it is in the blood that infects people is suppressed of killed by the oxygen that keeps us alive.

    As night turned into day this morning, I found some candy wrappers on the ground; a lot of them. Candy wrappers just like the ones back at the house. I was getting close.

    As I came out of the woods, I noticed a large building directly in front of me. Of course, it would have to be the one place to NEVER go during a zombie outbreak (according to Darrell)....a shopping mall!!!

Stupid kid.

I have been hanging around outside here for hours waitng to find a break between zombies so I can climb on to the roof. Once night falls, I will make my way up; if I can make it till night fall. This place is crawling with the ghouls.

Oh!

I need to go NOW!

There are no zombies around or none around that can get to me before I make it to the fire escape ladder. Sure they will see me, but they can't climb. I can make it....

Day 14

Shopping malls.

As if they aren't bad enough, now they are crawling with zombies. But if you think about it, weren't they always? I mean thousands of brain dead people wandering around aimlessly ready to bite your head off if you get too close to them. Very little difference. I almost feel safer now.

    Yesterday I saw an opening between a group of zombies and made a run for it; my ankle still throbbing from the fall a few days ago. When I got to the side of the building, I realized the ladder was much higher up than it had looked from the wood line. By the time I got there though, it was too late. I had committed and the zombies had spotted me. There was no turning back. Looking around, I had found an old metal dumpster that I could push under the ladder. By the time I managed to get the dumpster under the ladder and climb on top of it, I was completely surrounded by the undead. Their smell had gotten worse. The fumes were too much for me to stomach. As I began vomiting, my memories began taking me back to a time when I was a child playing in my father's barn. I flipped over a bale of hay to find a freshly rotting opossum. In my mind's eye, I could still see the maggots and worms covering the body. I opened my eyes so see the same site, but now they were covering the bodies of the living dead. Once I came back to my senses, I grabbed hold of my bat, pretending to play golf; I swung at the nearest zombie head I could find. He hit the ground about three feet away with a thud and a grunt. I didn't have to do it for my survival; I did it because I could. Those bastards have put me through hell, so now I plan on sending as many of them back there as I can.

    I made my way to the roof and found a door leading

into the mall. As I began walking down the stairs, I heard people talking and arguing. The closer I got, the louder they became. I turned the corner to see a group of people arguing about what to do with a young teen they had found wandering around in the mall. I glance around the room to see Cole sitting in the floor, curled up like a beaten dog. His eyes wide and unfocused, but overall, unharmed from what I could see.

    I was not going to allow these people to decide the fate of this kid, so I straightened myself, hid my bat, and approached the group slowly with my hands in the air. I had not made it three feet before they noticed my approach. After another three feet, I had five guns shoved in my face. One more step and I received a nice smack to the back of my head with what must have been the butt of a shotgun. When I awoke a few hours later, I could feel the nice golf ball size knot forming on the back of my skull. I opened my eyes to see the same group of people standing around me, this time though, no guns were drawn. After a few apologies from a very British sounding man, they began asking me questions about "the outside". What was it like now? Where were the safe places? Was I there to rescue them? Question after question was thrown my direction. I had no answers.

    After the barrage of unanswerable questions, I informed them I came for the boy and would be on my way after I rested. The group began arguing again, some wanted to go with me, others insisted I stay. Hours went by. Finally in the end, I had convened them to allow me to take the boy and we would leave the mall with anyone who dared go with us.

Cole slowly stood up and made his way over to the group. With hollow eyes, he looked directly at me, ignoring everyone else. "I had too. I mean, I just had to..." that was all he could say. There was nothing else he had to say.

We head out later tonight. I am taking Cole and three others. I can only pray I am not leading these sheep to their slaughter.

Day 15

Fallen ill.

Everything was set yesterday to leave the building. We had our new supplies, weapons, and even a hand drawn map for each of us in case we got separated from each other. We were ready. All I had to do was take that first step. I could not move. My body felt like hit had been hit with a dump truck. I felt feverish and had the sniffles. I knew it was a sinus infection...they did not. In fact, most of the group swore I had been bitten and was now infected. The group broke into a full blown fight over when to shoot me! I was surrounded by idiots. These people needed to be eaten alive. If all the guns weren't firmly planted in my direction, I would have run or even shot them all, but I couldn't. I was stuck, waiting for them to decide my fate....the fate of a man with a sinus infection.

After about half an hour, they came back with a decision. They would lock me (and now Cole, only because we knew each other) in a room until we changed, then they would shoot us! Great! My life is getting better by the second.

So here I sit, a prisoner wrongly imprisoned for having a runny nose. Cole imprisoned for just knowing me. I don't know, maybe it is better this way, after all, I am not much for taking out zombies in this condition. Plus, I could use a few days of sleep and rest. Thankfully, Cole doesn't say much, he knows the difference between a cold and "the change", so he is not worried either.
Well, I am feeling a little dizzy now, so I am going to lay down for a bit. I'll update ev

Wait!

Oh Christ! The zombies are in the mall! There must be hundreds or thousands of them in here! I have to get out of here. Cole is freaking out...We are like big old worms on a little bitty hook in here.

Day 16

They are still in here and so are we.

The beauty of being locked in a room is, even though we can't get out, they can't get in either. So here we sit, in a sort of stalemate. We are desperately trying to find a way out, while they are staring at us as if we were lobsters in a tank. It is only a matter of time before they break down the gate. The bottom is already starting to give way. I would say that within a matter of hours, they will be all over us. I just saw the three people that were going to leave with us. They are now zombies. Kind of funny how they were so worried about me, that they never realized they were about to turn themselves.
That's when I saw exactly what I was looking for! The keys to the room were hanging from the belt of one of them! All I had to do it get close enough to the gates to reach it, without getting bit. I had Cole distract them by banging on the gate and yelling for them to look his way. I can remember seeing people do this in movies and remember how funny I thought it was; as if it could actually happen, and yet here we were doing the exact same thing. I lay down on my stomach and crawled towards the gate and slowly reached up and grabbed the keys. When I tugged on the chain they were attached to, the zombie turned and looked directly at me. I yanked my hand down and back through the gate, practically ripping the undead guys pants off in the process; he didn't notice, they never do.

I am alive...for now, that's all I care about. I have the key and Cole has found a vent just big enough for him to crawl in to.
We have a plan!

Cole is going to crawl through the vent till he finds an opening. From there, he will distract the undead bastards. I will unlock the gate, sneak out of the room and make my way upstairs to the roof. Once I reach the roof, Cole will meet me there. We won't have much time, so we will have to climb down the ladder and make our way into the woods.

A long shot, yes, but it's our only shot. We have found some things we can use as weapons laying around in the room and I can see three guns on the ground right next to the room. We are ready.

Ok, Cole is in the vent...I need to sign off and get ready.

Day 17

I am exhausted! I am tired, sick as hell, beat up, cut up, bloodied, but alive and infection free. Cole is the same minus the sickness. I am only able to rest for a few minutes before we have to try to make our way back to our encampment. God I can't wait to get back. Sure the "fortress" is cramped, but it is safe.

The plan was working fine, Cole made a very nice distraction, just enough for me to unlock the door, squeeze out unnoticed, and grab the guns. What we didn't count on though was the one lone survivor of the other group. That stupid bitch just about got us all killed. Just as Cole was sliding back into the vent, out of nowhere this woman comes up behind me, screaming, crying, and begging me to take her with us. She was making such a fuss that every zombie within a one mile radius turned to look at us. You all have seen the movies where the nerdy white kids go into the predominately black bar and when they walk in, the music stops and everyone turns to look at them? This was the same reaction! I turned and screamed for her to "shut the hell up!" She stopped screaming and was caught off guard by my abruptness. As she stood facing me, she was frozen with fear and caught off guard just long enough for three zombies to rip into her neck and back with their teeth and nails. Blood covered me and everything around.

I ran. I ran faster than I had ever run before. I looked like a slalom skier, swerving back and forth avoiding the undead.

I reached the top floor before I ever had to use the gun. The sounds of the zombies head exploding were louder than the gun shot itself. I put the barrel of the gun directly at that bastard's nose and pulled the trigger. I am now getting a little concerned; I enjoy killing and hurting these things too much! That first shot was not the last, not by a long shot. I used every round I had for one of the guns. I believe it was a .45, regardless, it did its job.

Once I reached the roof, I was alone. Cole was nowhere in sight. I cursed under my breath. Bam! Bam! Bam! The vent burst open, with a very dirty Cole sliding out, coughing dust clouds. We had made it half way so far. We barricaded the door, so the zombies couldn't get on to the roof. I knew it wouldn't last long, but we did what we had to do. Next we ran over to the ladder, crawled down onto the dumpster. Zombies everywhere! We decided to just have fun with it. I handed Cole a gun (now I am not saying I believe in kids with guns, but during a zombie apocalypse, it is necessary). Together, we sent at least 20 of the back to hell. We jumped off the dumpster, running with everything we had in us. Once we got to the woods, we never turned back. We ran until we could no longer hear the dull moaning.

I have to rest some. My sickness is getting worse by the second. We will rest for just a few hours here, and then we will make our way back to safety. I cannot wait.

Day 18

They are all gone.

We arrived at the "safe house" early this morning, to find the place destroyed. The gate was pushed over and blood covered the ground and side of the house. Inside, the house was trashed and again, covered in blood. All the bodies were gone, except for a few zombies with smashed in faces lying around. It must have been a massacre.

As my mind wandered to Deanna, and how I hoped she had made it out in one piece and without getting bitten, I turned to see her standing in the doorway. This was not the Deanna I had left, not the Deanna who helped save me just a few days ago. This was her body, but everything else about her was gone. Most of the side of her face had been removed and she was missing an arm. She slowly shuffled towards me, moaning, with fresh blood streaming out of her mouth. She had eaten recently.

As I reached for my gun, Cole jumped in front of me. He would be the one to put his mother to rest. He slowly raised his gun, pointed it straight at his mother's head. I could hear him crying as he pulled the trigger. In a movie, this would have taken place in slow motion, but this was not a movie. This was real. Less than a second after he pulled the trigger, her head exploded into a huge puff of blood, skull, and brain matter. Her now lifeless body thudded onto the ground. Cole fell to the ground grasping her body. I could hear him whisper through the sobs "I love you mommy....I am sorry".

We buried her body under a tree beside the house and secured the gate. We will stay here for the night and leave in the morning. Cole has been asleep for a while now. God I hope I don't have to do that to Darcy when I find her, and I will find her.

Good night Deanna, you were like a sister to me. You will be missed.

Day 19

We couldn't go anywhere today. I am deathly ill. Cole is beginning to look at me funny. I think he is now thinking I am changing. I swear I am not. I will get better. I have to. Last night was quiet, almost too quiet. It is as if they know to leave us alone. Hell, I probably smell like death. I have been making plans in my head for our escape from this place. We will stick to the woods as much as possible. I don't know how far we can make it before we will have to stop for shelter, but we will walk until we cannot walk any more. Cole wants to find a car or a truck. That may be a good idea, but the streets are packed with cars. I think we will assess that situation when we get near roads. We have quite a few miles before we get to my home. I have no idea how bad it has gotten in other parts of the world. Maybe we will get lucky and this outbreak is getting better. I bet right now, scientists are putting the finishing touches on the antivirus as we speak. Yeah, wouldn't that be nice. Then the world would go back to the way we were. I would go back to my company and act like everything is normal. I can forget that I killed my supervisor with a fish bowl. Sure, I can forget it all.

Ok, I am delusional. My fever is getting worse. I can't stop throwing up. Oh God, what if I am changing?? How can this be?

I have to sleep now. I am so cold...

Day 20

Hi! I hope this works. My name is Cole. The guy that has been posting this is really sick right now. At least I hope he is just sick. He has been passed out all day. I hope he is going to be ok. He told me if he doesn't make it, to please continue this little project.

I am not much of a writer, in fact I have no idea what to write. I guess I should just go with what I am feeling. I am sad. I am scared. I am lonely. I don't know if I will make it out alive. But then, where is it I will go. I have seen some really bad stuff. I wish they would all go away. I have lost so many people I love and care about.

    Today, I saw three of my old friends, only they weren't my friends any more. Everyone around me calls them zombies. I think that's total bull crap though. I don't know what they are, but I know I am not stupid enough to call them zombies. Mom said they are just very sick. She told me to stay away from them. I should have listened to her. She should have taken her own advice, because she became one of them. All I know is that when someone gets bitten, they turn into one of them. Maybe it's a parasite, like that Superman comic I read or maybe it is Aliens like in that movie Invasion. That's my real theory. I think maybe they switched my mom and friends with alien counterparts. Maybe I will see my mom again soon. I have to stay alive so I can help them all.

    Why isn't he waking up? He is just moaning. I have my gun right here. If he isn't better in the next few hours, I will have to kill him to make sure he doesn't become one of them.

I can't wait any longer...

Day 21

Ok, so I didn't kill him last night. I was going to though. I approached him slowly, with my gun drawn and pointed at his head. I could tell he was still breathing, so obviously he wasn't one of those alien things yet. I sat in front of him all night long, waiting for his breath to stop, but it never did.

See, what I think happens are the aliens are stopping time and somehow switching the bodies really fast. That's why the people are breathing one minute but not the next. I think the illness people get is like a slow moving poison or something that prepares the people for transportation. It takes the aliens a few minutes to restart their new bodies, so I knew if he stopped breathing, the switch would have been made and I would have just a couple minutes before I would have had to kill him (or it).

Hey, maybe that's it, I remember my uncle letting me stay up late one night and watch a scary movie. We watched the movie "The Thing". Man, I was so scared. But now I'm thinking that's could be what's going on. I wonder if I should test our blood. I'll try that and come right back.

Alright, I just figured out two things. First, getting blood from your finger hurts! Secondly, I learned that he is not one of them. Not from the blood test, but from the fact that he punched me right in the nose and yelled at me for sticking a pin in his finger. He called me a stupid kid. He said something about feeling better, but that he was just tired now and needed more sleep. He also said in order for him to be a (he called it a zombie again), but in order to be one of those things, he would have to be bitten and he was clearly not bitten. Then he told me to shut up and let him sleep. I think he's going to be ok.

    I'm not sure where we are going to go once he is better. He kept talking about some chick he was supposed to marry. I think her name was Dercie, or Darcy or something like that. He wants to get back to her. I personally think she is probably one of them now and going after her would be a mistake. Whatever we do, I think we should at least find a car. I hope we can find a sweet Honda or some kind of awesome turbo car. I am just tired of walking. I think I may go out and find a car, so when he wakes up it is already sitting there waiting on us. Yeah, I am going to go ahead and do that. I think he will be really happy when he finally wakes up, to find a car already packed and ready. I'll show him I'm not a stupid kid.

Day 22

    That stupid kid went to get a car while I was out of it! I thought I was dying for a few days. But I awoke today alone in this abandoned house of death. It's no wonder I have been so sick. All the dead people wandering around, plus all the rain I had been wandering around in. I am feeling a little better now though. I am still very weak and don't think I can go anywhere. I hope that little idiot blocked the gates! I am not going to go looking for him this time. He got into this mess; he can get himself out of it. I don't want anything to happen to him, but I can't battle the undead today...and YES, they are zombies not some alien invasion. I would think the rotting flesh would have tipped him off to this fact. Maybe I will run into him somewhere down the road soon. I hope I don't run into his little ass as a zombie, I kind of liked the kid; don't want to have to shoot him, plus there's the promise I made to his mother.

So I guess if I am feeling a little better tomorrow, I will leave here. I have to make my way home. I had dreams about being at home. They were more like nightmares. In my dream, I walked to the front door, where I was greeted by Darcy; still as beautiful as the day I met her. She greeted me with a hug and a kiss. It was a very sweet kiss. We stood face to face, holding each other, our bodies intertwined into one; noses brushing against each other as we stared into each other's eyes. We were in love like no one has ever been in love before. We began to kiss again. This time it was a long deep kiss, however, this time, she began sucking on my mouth. I couldn't breathe. She was sucking the air out of my body. When I finally pulled away, she was a zombie. Her face was still perfect, except for her eyes; they were a stone white color with a dark black pupil that seemed to rip its way into my soul; the rest of her body quickly decamped right in front of me. She screamed and begged me to come to her. I couldn't help but walk towards her, slowly, gasping for air. I reached for her. When I touched her, she turned into powder. I screamed in horror. As the feeling of loss overwhelmed me, I collapsed onto her ashes. As I lay there weeping and mourning her loss, a cold hand slowly wrapped around my neck. I turned to see the perfect now angelic Darcy standing there before me, wearing all white. She approached me and with her pale soft hand easily picked me up by the throat and turned me toward her. I couldn't breathe. She stared into my eyes and told me she loved me. She then pulled me close to her and sunk her perfect teeth into my neck. I laid there as she devoured my body, pulling the flesh off and ripping the muscles from the bone. I was unable to move; unable to fight for my life. She saved my face for last; so I could see what she was doing. Just as she began to rip my eyes out, I woke up. I have had this dream twice now. What could it mean?

I am feeling weak again. I have to rest some more. I need to rest so I can leave tomorrow...

I hear someone screaming!?!

God, its Cole! He is close and getting closer.

Day 23

We have added two more people to our little group, thanks to Cole.

So yesterday, when Cole was screaming, I crawled out of bed and made my way to the front gate as quickly as a sick person could. By the time I got to the gate, Cole was banging on it as hard as he could, but he was not alone. In fact, there were three people with him. They were screaming and banging on the gate, begging for me to open it. As I opened the gate, Cole forced his way past me, panting and white as a ghost. Behind him, a cute blond was being pulled into the front by a guy who looked to be military. The last person was a brunette female. She was limping and crying; she was a good ways behind the others and looked as though she had been bitten many times. Directly behind her were what appeared to be about 20 zombies. Because of her slow pace, the monsters were quickly upon her. One of them reached out and snagged her by her long curly hair. The sudden stopping of her head, made her feet fly out from underneath her. She landed on the ground with a heavy thump! Four zombies fell on top of her. They began making a meal out of her face and arms. She screamed until they ripped out her vocal cords, then the only sounds we heard were the crunching of bones, and the distinct sounds of teeth ripping flesh from muscle. I quickly closed the door. God, I have seen too much of this kind of brutality.

46

As I turned to the group, the blond (Tonya) was hysterical. She was sobbing and asking for Mary. I later found out from Ken (the military guy), that Tonya and Mary were lovers. They had met years ago and were together when the uprising began. Apparently, Tonya and Mary had met Ken while they were escaping the city. They had been on the run, but their car got stuck in some mud while maneuvering around stalled cars on the side of the road. While Ken and Mary had gotten behind the car to push it out of the mud, Tonya stayed in to help steer and maneuver. Out of nowhere, Mary was grabbed and bitten quite a few times, before Ken could pull her to safety in the car. Cole heard the commotion and came to the rescue. He shot four zombies that were surrounding the car, which gave the three the opportunity to escape. Before they could get very far, the gun shots attracted even more attention. They ran as fast as they could towards the house. Tonya tried to help Mary as much as she could, but knowing that her fate was already sealed, Ken pulled her on ahead.

After hearing the story from Ken, we all rested.

W e awoke this morning to find Tonya standing by the gate. Her head was down; tears streamed down her face, her right hand clutched a picture of her and Mary, her left hand pressed against the gate. I allowed her to say her last good byes, before I called a meeting. We discussed a strategy for staying alive. We decided to work as a team. We would not kill any zombies unless we had to so we wouldn't cause any undue attention. We had to find a safer location before every zombie with in 100 square miles was upon us. W e agreed to split up and gather supplies in the house and meet back just before dark under the tree where Deanna was buried. This was Cole's idea. He wanted to say good bye one last time to his mother.

Tonya was upset, and rightfully so. She had just seen the love of her life ripped apart before her eyes. She wanted revenge! It took a little convincing, but in the end, she agreed that Mary would have wanted her to live and be happy. I promised that when the opportunity came up to kill one of the undead, she would get the first chance...hell, she could kill them with her bare hands if she wanted to, and I think she just might.

Ken is a very quite person. He hasn't said much about his past. I only know he used to be in the Navy. I am going to try to find out more about him. I am glad he is with us. I need someone strong beside me.
We have a good team. I am confident we will make it to a new safe house without any problems. I am just hoping our next safe house will be my house...

Day 24

Ken's Story.

Since nothing exciting happened throughout the night, other than seeing quite a few large groups of zombie pass by us, I thought I would tell you Ken's story as he relayed it to me.

Ken was in the Navy for eight years as an aircraft mechanic. When he got out, he secured a well paying job with a huge airline company. A few weeks before the "uprising", he was laid off from the job. Getting laid off from his dream job sent him into a huge depression. He said he wanted to end his life. He had planned on taking a hand full of pills and drinking himself into a coma that he would never wake from. He put on his best suit, left notes for all his friends and family, and gathered a bottle of Xanax pills and a bottle of Jack Daniels. He sat on his bed and placed all the pills into his mouth; that's when the phone rang. He decided to answer it, after all, maybe he could tell someone good bye before he finished himself off. On the other end of the phone, was someone calling for a job interview in the city. The pay and benefits were much better than what he was making and he was very qualified for the position. He decided to wait to find out about the job before offing himself.

A few days before the interview, he said he

remembered watching the news about that Shawn kid coming back from the dead, but didn't think much of it. The day of the interview, the city was total chaos; however, he was not going to let anything stop him from making that interview. When he got to the building, he realized something was very wrong. People were running all over the place and being chased by other people covered in blood.

Ken said it was like a light bulb going off. Something was definitely wrong. People were being eaten alive on the streets right in front of him. He decided to skip the interview – for obvious reasons. As he began leaving the city, he saw two women trapped in a burning car that was surrounded by "these things" (as he called them). He grabbed for his tire iron and went to rescue the women. When he approached the car, two of the "things" turned around just in time to get a nice piece of iron implanted into their skulls. The last two slowly walked towards him. With one downward swing, the tire iron crushed the head in of one of them, and with a powerful uppercut, he nearly removed the head of the other one. He got the women out of the car and ran for safety. They took shelter in an old warehouse that was scheduled to be torn down within the next few weeks. They stayed there the next few weeks, scavenging for food and water whenever it was safe. Ken felt like he had a purpose; a reason to live again. He needed these women to be ok.

They fled the city two days ago, when their warehouse had become compromised. They found an exit and made their way to Ken's car and headed out of the city as fast as they could. That is when Cole found them.
I like Ken. I think he will be one hell of an ally. A man with a purpose for living is not a man to mess with.

Day 25

    I awoke this morning to the sounds of Ken and Cole arguing over whether or not we should get a car. It was getting pretty heated, until Tonya ran over and separated them. Cole wanted to get a car, Ken did not. They both had very valid points, but I am sick of walking, so my vote was for the car. Tonya cast her vote with Ken, so we were dead locked. No one would budge on the issue. I know Tonya wanted a car, but Ken saved her life, so she felt like she owed him something. It's not that I was on Cole's side; it's just that my lazy ass did not want to walk any more. We all stood there in an old tool shed we had found in someone's back yard, facing each other, tempers were rising. I guess the sounds of arguing had attracted the attention of some nearby zombies, because before any of us knew it, the building was completely surrounded. The zombies began banging on the walls outside, desperately trying to get inside. We had no way of knowing how many were out there because of the lack of windows in the shed, but we knew there were quite a few.

    Panic began to set in. How could we all make it out without getting bit? The odds were stacked against us. I glanced around the shed, looking for "the perfect weapon". We were running short on bullets and needed something; anything to take out the undead bastards and clear a path for our escape. Cole grabbed an old rusty machete with Duck tape on the handle. Ken and I both grabbed for the chainsaw hanging on the wall. There was no time to argue, so I reluctantly let him have it. Tonya grabbed a garden hoe from the corner and prepared for battle. I looked around for something that I could use. That's when I had found what I would use. Underneath an old blue tarp was a little red push mower just small enough for me to pick up.

    I grabbed the mower, blades facing out. Ken pulled the cord with my hands carefully gripping the sides, I kicked open the door and blindly ran out. Within seconds, I had "mowed" down three of them. Their bodies sliced in half with ease. The amount of old rancid blood covering my body was amazing. I was swinging the mower from side to side slicing and dicing the undead as if they were weeds in a yard. I turned to my left to clear a path for the others. I was completely blind, swinging the lawn mower from side to side, hitting anything in my path. That's about the time when I stepped on the entrails of one of my sliced zombies. I hit the ground with a thud, the mower falling on top of me, crushing one of my ribs. Thankfully the engine must have flooded, because it shut off as soon as I hit the ground. I shoved it off to one side and quickly scrambled to my feet. I was looking around, admiring my trail of blood and guts, when an old dried hand wrapped around my arm. I my stomach sank. I all I heard was the moaning. I could feel the anticipation radiating through him and could smell his rancid breath getting closer to my head. No one was around to save me. I could feel my legs getting weak as I braced for the bite.

It never came.

I heard the moaning stop with a sudden crack. I turn around to see some big guy pounding the zombie in the face with a wooden bat. He was huge and wore an orange skull cap, a Rob Zombie t-shirt, camouflage shorts and a fanny pack. He was a very strange looking man. He stopped crushing the monsters head in and looked directly at me. All I could think to say was "thanks". He rolled his eyes and motioned for me to follow him. Together we went to help my friends.

The others were busy hacking and slashing their own zombies. Tonya had a little smile on her face every time her hoe would plant itself into one of their heads. Ken and I had to pull her off one of the corpses she had just mauled in order for us to leave. She was crying and cursing as she jammed the hoe in and out of the lifeless body on the ground. She got her revenge this day.

When the "battle" was over, we all followed the strange tall man to his "home".

His house was an old two story home converted into a full time haunted house complete with ghosts and ghouls hanging in the trees as well as a small fake cemetery near the front door. The stranger introduced himself as Spook. He told us about how it was always his dream to run a haunted house. Horror movies were his favorite. He told us about his wife Paula that went to the grocery store when the major outbreak began, but never returned home.
Spook cooked a warm meal of rice and pork and beans for us. God, it was so good to eat a warm meal again. Even though it is kind of strange being in a house surrounded by fake dead people, it feels safe.

Thank you Spook for your kindness.

You get your dream, not only do you have a house full of zombies, you get a world full of them too.

Day 26

We went on a tour of the haunted house today. I don't know which is scarier, this house or being outside with the undead. The house is crazy; with monsters that jump out from walls and other assorted haunts hanging from ceilings and in staged "death" scenes. Maybe it is because of what has been going on lately, but I was in no mood to go through this place. I left the house early and wandered around the back area, behind the scenes. It was a pretty neat set up he had going. While I was wondering around, I came across a room. This room was full of guns! Every type of gun you could imagine. There were even grenades and LAW rockets lying around in boxes. This Spook guy was ready for a war. While I was looking around, Spook came into the room. He seemed a little irritated at me discovering his "stash" as he called it. He asked me to leave the room immediately. I asked him how long he had been collecting the weapons. He responded with "quite a while, even before the zombies...I was afraid of the terrorists". He just smiled. I know we were both laughing a little inside. Hell, I wish it were the terrorists we were fighting; at least they don't bite you and turn you into one of them.

After seeing the room, I suddenly feel much safer now.

Today was another quiet day. Maybe we are thinning out the undead population. Maybe they are starving themselves to death. I wonder how many normal people there are still out there.

I really like being here, but I am going to leave tomorrow. I have somewhere to go. I am on a mission. Nothing is going to keep me from getting home.

Day 27

Miracles and Curses.

The word of the day yesterday was arguments. All night it was a battle between all of us. I was leaving, no matter who liked it or not. Cole decided he would follow me anywhere. Tonya and Ken wanted to stay with Spook and wanted us to stay as well. "She's dead...get over it" was all they could say to me. They told me it was suicide to travel through the city with just myself and a 14 year old kid. I was pissed. No one would tell me where I could and could not go. My decision had been made and would not let anyone tell me differently. Cole and I would leave first thing in the morning. W e spent the remainder of the night packing up and gathering supplies from the house.

Sometime around 7:30 a.m. this morning, Cole and I were saying our goodbyes to everyone when we heard a truck horn blaring somewhere off in the distance. It was a semi truck, just the cab, and no trailer. It was headed straight for the house. Following quicker than I thought they should, was a group of close to 1000 zombies. The truck came to a stop inches from the front door. Out of the cab came three people. They were bloodied, bruised, and starving, but they were alive.

The first out was a young boy that appeared to be barely older than Cole, behind him was a girl around my age. She was wearing a shirt with a name tag that read "Hi! My name is Erin". The "i" in the name Erin had a little smile face on top instead of the dot. The last person out of the truck was the miracle that gives me more hope than I have ever gotten. Spooks wife, gone for over three weeks, crawled out of the drivers' side door. Spook dropped to his knees crying. There was no time for the reunion though, no sooner did Paula step out of the truck, than the horde of the undead was upon us. We ran inside the house, in just enough time to get the door shut and blocked.

Spook and Paula embraced just inside front of the door. I ran to the weapons room. Once inside, I grabbed as many guns and as much ammo as I could carry and ran back to the foyer. Tonya was hysterical; Cole kept an eye on the back of the house. I threw Ken a shot gun and rifle. Spook got his M -16 from behind the coat rack. (Yes, this man keeps a machine gun behind the coat rack!) I passed out the remaining weapons to everyone else. We were ready for anything.

The rest of today we have been waiting inside, taking pot shots at a few zombies stupid enough to get near a window. The house is very secure. They cannot get in. My fear though is how long we will have to stay here, trapped like rats. Every hour more and more zombies show up. They are all shapes and sizes. I have seen babies barely old enough to crawl, covered in dry blood, next to the extreme elderly, pulling themselves across the ground, no longer able to use the wheelchair that moved them from place to place when they were alive. This virus, this plague, this curse does not discriminate. It does not care about wealth or stature, everyone is at risk and now we are completely surrounded by them as more show up.

It seems I will never get home. Darcy may be alive. She may be ok, but if I cannot get out of here, I may never know. I am trapped. I cannot leave. I must be cursed.

Day 28

We have spent the better part of the day shooting the zombies that have surrounded the house. I haven't had this much fun in years. I guess that's kind of a bad thing to admit. "Hi! I am an addict....I am addicted to shooting people in the head". I must have killed 100 of them today so far. We decided to crawl onto the roof just to get a better idea of how many were out there. I was shocked! I lost count there were so many. It was amazing. I even saw an old neighbor of mine. His name was Rey. He used to be in a band...really nice guy. I think he was the singer. Though after taking an M -16 bullet to the head, I doubt he will ever sing again! The first shot grazed his shoulder. He barely flinched. The second shot took off his jaw. Finally the third shot removed the entire back half of his head. I couldn't help but laugh to myself. First my dog shits in his yard, and then I blow off his head!

Ken, Cole, Spook, and the new kid Brett, all enjoyed taking turns blasting the women they saw. Erin, Paula, and Tonya all stood around watching, though they all participated. In all, we took out close to 500 of them. Their bodies littering the ground, making a nice body fence around the house.

Spook spent most of his time with Paula. They barely moved from each other's side. I know Darcy and I will be the same. We will not want to be away from each other for even a second. This is the longest we have been apart since the "invasion". Let me tell you, it is true; absence does make the heart grow fonder.

Ken has promised to show us later how to throw a grenade. I remember throwing one when I was in the military, but that was so long ago. I have always wanted to see what it will do to a person, tonight I will get that chance.

Brett and Cole have become close friends over the past few hours. Hell, they could be brothers. They laugh at the same things, and talk for hours about video games they have played and girls they used to know. It is kind of strange how things work out. Three and a half weeks ago, I never wanted kids, now here I am taking care of two teenagers. How did I get put in charge anyway?

Well, it looks like we are going back on the roof. Erin wants to do more shooting. She is out there waiting for us. She looks so happy. I don't know much about her, she is so quiet. Maybe I can find out more tonight.

Oh my God!

She fell off the roof

Day 29

They ripped that poor girl to shreds. I guess maybe they were taking revenge for what we had done to their kind. Hell, they are brain dead, all they think about is eating; eating us that is. The creepy thing is after they had eaten most of her, she began to twitch. She then rose up from the ground; all the meat missing from both arms, her left leg had been completely ripped off at the knee, but she still managed to get up. She would rise up on one leg, try to take a step, then fall, face first onto the ground. It reminded me of a bee trying to fly out a closed window. No matter how hard she tried, she just couldn't get anywhere. We all just watched her for about an hour. Ken finally stepped up. He got down on one knee, aimed his rifle just right, for a proper kill. He asked if anyone wanted to say something, like a memorial. We all kept our mouths shut. No one knew her. It's not that we didn't care about her, but after everything we have all been through, watching someone, anyone, die like that, didn't mean much to us. I guess we have become desensitized by this experience. Ken closed one eye, placed her head directly in his sites and slowly squeezed the trigger. Erin's head exploded like a watermelon with an M -80 firecracker in it. She never got up again.

The rest of the night, we all sat in silence...well, it would have been silent had it not been for the moaning of the undead directly outside the house. Their constant moaning can really wear on your nerves. Is it the hunger that makes them moan or some kind of biological release of air through the lungs? Either way, it is beginning to annoy me again. I mean we are trapped here; unable to go anywhere and all they can do is moan. I think it is having an impact on everyone now. We are all on edge.

Arguments spring up almost every hour. We are arguing over stupid things like who turned on the light, or who didn't flush the toilet. Ken is becoming very restless. He has been pacing back and forth across the hall way for the past 3 hours. I am getting sick of looking at all these fake zombies and monsters. I wish I could have found somewhere else to stay. Why couldn't a nice old lady have found us? Instead, I am stuck with this lunatic. I am stuck with all the lunatics. I can't breathe. I feel claustrophobic. Why won't that moaning go away??

Spook is screaming at Cole and Brett in the other room; something about touching his fog machine. Tonya is just sitting in the corner rocking back and forth. Paula is humming some old song. Why won't she shut the hell up??? The moaning is bad enough.

This place is turning into a ticking time bomb. I am afraid something really bad is going to happen very soon...

Day 30

One month! This has been going on for one month! One month ago today I woke up, kissed Darcy good bye and headed to work. Sure I knew about all the strange stuff going on around the world, but hey, isn't there always? Honestly, I never really watched the news and on my way to work that day, I was listening to my IPod. It wasn't until I got to work that I heard about everything going on in the city. Now that I think back, I do remember seeing quite a few people walking down the road. I also remember seeing a lot of police cars and ambulances that morning, but in the city, you see that all the time. I should have stayed home. Had I stayed home, I wouldn't be sitting in this Hell hole of a house.

Spook won't shut up about the lack of food and has now started yelling at Paula on a regular basis. Ken and Cole have to stay in different rooms to keep from killing each other and Brett has been hitting on Tonya all morning poor kid doesn't realize he is barking up the wrong tree. I just keep looking out the window, through a couple boards fastened to the inside. It allows me just enough room to see the front of the house. The moaning is getting worse with each passing minute. It is driving us all insane. Tonya tried calming everyone down today, by telling jokes, but no one seemed to care. It was not a time to laugh. She told some joke about two guys walking into a bar, but I forget the punch line; must not have been too funny.

Spook is right to worry about food though; we are running out! We have enough to last maybe one more day, if we don't eat much. Two teenagers can clean out a house full of food within hours and we have been here for days. If we don't leave here soon, we will not have to worry about the zombies, we will die of hunger.

I think tonight I will get on the roof and try to take out more of those bastards. I have to do something. If nothing else, it will stop a few more from moaning. Aghhh please let that moaning stop! I can hear Brett screaming at them to shut up from another room. I have to go calm him down...if I can calm myself down.

Day 31

We are out of food. Someone broke into the pantry last night and ate it all! I think it was Brett or Cole. They are two teenage boys who could eat an elephant. Spook is pissed, just as we all are. What are we going to do for food now? This is all we need. We are all going a little insane and now someone ate all the food. The constant moaning outside is still there, mocking us, taunting us, begging us to come outside and look for food. I will come out with a rocket to shove up their asses!

I am feeling so claustrophobic in here...even when I get on the roof, I feel locked in. For every ten zombies we kill, 20 more pop up. I have no doubt they will break through our barricades soon. You can hear the wood creaking and cracking from inside. One good push and they would be in. They are literally squeezing the house like a zit. We have begun taking shifts on the roof...safely on the roof. If it looks like they are breaking through, the watcher will yell for everyone. We have no escape plan though. My suggestion is to move to the roof. It is hard enough for us to get to, so I am sure it would be impossible for the brain dead to get to us. We wouldn't last up there long though; the lack of food and water would kill us.

The only plan I have would involve somehow getting all the zombies on one side of the house, then someone making a mad dash for the truck that Paula drove to get here. I have no way to get all the zombies to one side though. Hell, getting down there would be a death wish for anyone....not that the truck would hold all of us anyway. I made some signs and put them on the roof; in case a helicopter happens to fly by; maybe they will see we are alive. Doubtful, though, I haven't seen anything in the sky in weeks. No planes, or helicopters hell, I haven't even seen and birds. My guess is they are all down on the ground, picking the flesh off the dead. So much food, their little fat bellies are probably too full to fly! God, I wish I had that problem right now. I guess that's the irony here, humans are the ones that normally have plenty of food, while everything else starves, now we are starving, while everything else gets it's fill.

Tonya is inside, trying to keep everyone's minds off of food; I don't think it's working though. Spook does not look amused, neither does Paula. Ken is playing investigator trying to figure out who ate all the food. He is closely looking for clues, like that show C.S.I. (that I used to watch). To him, everyone is a suspect. Brett and Cole are wrestling around in the living room, next to a 10 foot tall Frankenstein. I am sitting here, tapping away at the keyboard. I can hear bellies rumbling over the moaning from outside. I haven't gone into panic mode yet, but I can feel it coming.

Day 32

We are trying to come up with a plan to get out of here. However, the problem with coming up with a plan, is we are all very hungry and can't think straight. We also can't seem to agree on anything. Spook wants to throw a few grenades and shoot a LAW rocket at the crowd, to clear out enough for one of us to make it to the truck. Ken wants to do my plan of detracting them so one of us can sneak to the truck. Brett and Cole both agree with Spook, but only because they want to see the explosions. Tonya is indifferent; she wants to stay here and see what happens. Paula has not said a word since last night, after a huge fight between Spook and herself.

I spent the majority of last night reinforcing the barricades throughout the house. I have no doubt they will break through tomorrow, if not tonight. We have every piece of furniture strapped and hammered to the walls and windows. The only way to see outside is from the roof.

Anything that is not bolted to the ground has been used. At least once an hour I can hear them breaking through. When you have thousands of zombies surrounding the small place you're in, eventually something is going to break. It is just a matter of time before they are in here tearing us to shreds.

I can hear them all around us. I think it would be safer for us to move up to the roof now. That way, when they break through, we will have a little time to....

I hear a truck outside! It sounds like it is getting closer...who the Hell could be out there??

I have moved up to the roof now. Some idiot is driving a truck through the yard, running over all the zombies! I have never seen so much blood! He must have hit 1000 of them. This guy is psychotic! He is hanging his head out of the cab cheering for himself! He can barely keep the truck moving in a straight line because of all the blood and guts that are now covering the ground like snow in the winter time.

Who would have thought, our salvation this time would come in the form of a crazy long haired guy in a Mac truck! I have to go get some weapons. It looks like we might be on the road again!

Day 33

Oh thank God we are out of that house, even if we are with a true nut job. The mysterious truck driver, who goes by the name Malice, said he had been driving down the road, when he saw my signs I put on the roof. He said he wanted to wait for just the right moment to come get us. I guess for him, the right moment was when 2000 zombies were surrounding the house! After he went on his driving rampage, he backed the truck into the house. Yes, literally into the house. We scraped off all the chunks of zombie meat and bone, opened the back of the truck and all piled in as fast as we could. Once we were in, Malice pulled out as fast as he could, though it was a slippery ride. The amount of blood and crushed bodies were staggering. Hands and legs were moving on their own along the ground like hundreds of ants.

We got quite a few miles down the road before he pulled the truck over. When the door flew open, we were greeted by a scruffy looking guy. He had long black hair and a long black beard to match. He said he was a truck driver and was just trying to get home. He lived hundreds of miles away from where we were. He said he had a girlfriend back home he was trying to get to. (It seems we all have someone to get home to.) He said he had been in Texas delivering something for the government when all hell broke loose. He told us how he was staying with his brother Jay and his wife Kellie in Texas after he made his drop. He said they were held up in the house for days before the zombies finally broke through their barricades. He described in great detail how Jay fought off what seemed like a hundred before he was finally over powered and mauled. He told how Kellie was so devastated at what she had just seen happen to her husband that she ran towards Jay, only to be eaten alive within seconds. He said right then and there, he would make a pact to kill as many of them as he could, on his way back to his girl Seras. He said in total, he has taken out more than 3000. Hell, probably most of them at our safe house.

I am not sure what to make of this Malice guy. He may be just a guy that is upset at the way things have gone, but to me, he seems more like a serial killer. The guy just stares at me, like he knows who I am and what I have done. Maybe it's just me though. I do have to have to cut him a little slack though; he did bring quite a bit of food. He had been stopping here and there at different places, stocking up of supplies. We ate really well last night and this morning.

It wasn't until earlier this afternoon that I realized we were going the wrong way! We were heading away from the city! I needed to go through the city to get to my house! Now I am even further away than when I started. Now don't get me wrong, I am very thankful for him rescuing us, but now what?!

We have been sitting in one spot the majority of the

day. We are on top of a hill, that way we can see either direction. We are also debating as to what to do. I will not waver on my feelings. We go back through the city to get Darcy! End of discussion. I will go with or without the psychotic Malice guy. Spook and Paula want to stay with him. That figures! Two people with Halloween names want to stick together. Ken and Tonya don't really want to go back to the city, but they get creeped out by the truck driver also. Brett and Cole said they will follow me where ever I go. We are going to talk about it more after we eat.

Tonya just said she heard a noise in the bushes! We are going to investigate...

Day 34

It was the hardest thing I ever had to do.

We found in the bushes a little boy. He was no older than six months or a year old; he was a zombie. He just lay on the ground, arms so still he could not move them other than to flail them around. He moaned and looked at us...he wanted to eat us. My guess is his mother or father put him there to hide him from the zombies, unaware he was already infected, or maybe they knew he was infected and put him there, unable to do what needed to be done; what we knew needed to be done.

The decision was easy; it was the act that was not. Paula wanted to just leave him there. Malice wanted to "bash his brains against a Goddamn radiator". We had to make it quick. Leaving him there to starve was inhumane. What if someone came across him and got bit by him? Then we would have one more zombie to worry about. No, it had to be done. But who would do it? We all voted that Malice would have nothing to do with this. Spook and Paula wanted nothing of it. I did not want Brett or Cole to have this looming over their head for the rest of their lives. So it was between Ken, Tonya, and myself.

I found some pieces of hay close by and cut one of them shorter than the others. We decided the only way was to draw straws. Cole mixed the hay up and held it in his hand. We all drew to see who would end the life of this child. Ken drew first, then Tonya, then me. My piece of hay matched Kens.

Tonya drew the short "straw".

She asked us all to leave her alone with him. I gave her a shotgun. I didn't want any mistakes. We all walked away from them. I could hear Tonya talking to the little boy.

She told him she was sorry, she begged for forgiveness, then she shot him.

The rest of the night, we all sat in total silence. What

was there to say? May God forgive us.

Day 35

    Last night while we were asleep, Malice thought it would be a good idea to just leave. Normally I would not have cared, but we were in the trailer of the truck. We all awoke to the rumble of the engine and the sudden take off. The bastard locked us in "for our own good", and took off for home. He said he knew going back to the city was suicide and he would not let us do that. We were banging on the walls trying to get his attention and trying to get him to stop. That's when I heard him let out a whoop as he ran over groups of living dead. Every time he would run over a few, it would knock us around. He began swerving to hit them. The truck would violently yank to the left or the right, and then we would feel the familiar bump and hear the hoot from Malice. As much fun as this was for him, we were getting pretty banged up.

    During one violent yank, the truck tipped sideways as it had a few times before, only this time, he could not recover. The truck began to flip sideways, like someone rolling a brick down a hill. We must have flipped three of four times before coming to a stop against a building.

    The truck bed was ripped in half. Myself, Cole, and

Tonya were in one side; Brett, Spook, Paula, and Ken were in the other side. I lay on the wall which was now the floor of the truck, where I landed, until I heard Paula screaming and crying. I jumped up, blood rushing down my arm from a large cut on my shoulder. As I looked around, I saw Cole and Tonya helping each other up. They appeared to be ok, just a little banged up. I jumped out of the trailer and made my way over to the other side. Paula was holding the now lifeless body of Brett, his neck contorted in a very unnatural way. Spook was behind her, trying to help Ken, who was trapped, penned between two pieces of the trailer. His leg was crushed. Blood flowed freely from just above his knee. He was pale and almost completely unresponsive. I ran over to Spook, trying in vain to pull back the metal. The more we worked, then more damage we were causing. Now, as if to mock us even more, Cole began yelling something about zombies coming. I ran to look. He was right; a massive group had obviously heard our wreck and was coming after their meal. We had a decision to make. Do we leave him here, or pull him, no matter how much damage was done. Either way, we had to go. Ken made the decision for us. He reached down and grabbed the gun Spook had in his belt. He told us to go. He said he was dead either way.

We left Brett's body lying next to Ken. As we ran into the nearest building, we could hear Ken shooting multiple times, then nothing but silence.

There we stood, all of us bloodied and banged up.

Tonya tended my wounds while Cole sat in the corner crying for his lost friend. Spook and Paula held each other and kept watch. Malice was gone; nowhere to be seen. I swear to God if I ever see that man again, I will blow is fucking head off.

How much more can we take??

Day 36

The power has been going off and on all day. I guess that is just one more problem to add on to our growing number. Tonya made some makeshift stitches for my arm. The pain was almost unbearable. I had to bite down on a stick to keep from screaming. Tonya has been a life saver to me; I want to get to know her a little better. Every day I like her more and more. I truly believe she would do anything for any of us. She sat next to me and talked most of the night. She told me so much about her past, but it just made me want to know more...or do I? Should I even try to get close to anyone ever again? It seems as if every time I get close to someone, they end up dead.

Other than Tonya talking to me, there was no one else even saying a word. After what we have been through, there was not much to say. We saw quite a few zombies walk (if that's what you call it) past the building we were in, but none of them even glanced in our direction. That is a good thing, since I would not be able to offer any help. Our plan is to just keep quiet and stay put for a few days. We are all bruised pretty good and could use the break. Earlier today I thought I saw a quick glimpse of Malice (what a VERY fitting name). He was running between a couple buildings. He looked like a scared cat, trying to stay hidden. He needs to stay out of my way if he knows what's good for him.

    I have no idea where we are. I know we're not in the city....we are in a small town. This building we are in is a two story office building. It looks like the company was some kind of ad agency. There are banners and signs everywhere. A Huge sign sitting in the corner reads "A+ Paws and Claws inc." another one is for some place called "Nanny's and More". Sitting in a printer is an unfinished sign that reads "Dine and Dash Auto Clea". There is quite a bit of blood on the ground near the printer. No doubt the worker was probably attacked as they were working. Upstairs there are quite a few offices and a large break room. Everything in the fridge is rotten.

    Back downstairs, Spook and Paula are huddled in a corner. I am worried about Paula. She hasn't stopped crying since yesterday. She has a wild look in her eyes. We need to watch her...she may try to do something stupid. In extreme situations like this, it is not unusual for someone to…

Someone is coming through the back door! I can't see if it is a zombie or a live person. Spook is on his feet, pistol in hand, Tonya is right by his side.
Oh my God, it's Ken...

Day 37

Ken is alive.

After we walked away from the accident, he held the gun close. He said most of the zombies tried following us, but the few that came after him got a face full of lead. He told us about how he knew he was done for and almost shot himself, but decided to go out fighting. He said when he got to the last bullet, there were about five zombies remaining. They were moving towards him, ready to eat, when out of nowhere, Malice appeared behind the undead bastards. Ken said Malice was wildly swinging a metal pipe at their heads. Within seconds, he had them all laying in a big bloody mess at his feet. Ken told how Malice helped free him from the wreckage with a crowbar he found in the cab of the truck. Once he was free, he took shelter in the wreckage until it was safe to come out. He said that Malice felt so bad about what had happened, he could not and would not face any of us. Malice had saved Ken from certain death then ran off into the shadows. It is hard to remain mad at someone who would help, but at the same time, he is to blame for the death of a 15 year old boy. Ken may be safe from the zombies, but his leg is severely mangled. I don't think he will last much longer with that wound. We have stopped the bleeding, but if infection sets in, he will die within days. The most we can do it is watch it and try to keep it clean. If he does make it, he will never walk right again; maybe in the "old" days when we had hospitals, but not now....not in this mess.

I found a map of the local area and have decided to go looking for a hospital, or that dog place I saw on the sign "A+ Paws and Claws", maybe they have some kind of antibiotics. I don't see a hospital on the map, but maybe I can find a doctor's office. If not, then Ken, you're getting dog medicine.

Day 38

Spook and I decided to be the ones to go looking for medicine. We gathered what little supplies we could find, plus the map, and headed out. Finding the hospital was easy. In fact, we were there before dark last night. The hard part will be getting into it without being seen. It seems the zombies flock to hospitals, probably because that's where the living head to when something is wrong.

This is a small town, so the hospital isn't very big.

The whole building is no bigger than a small warehouse. We are in a house directly across the street from the emergency room entrance. Three ambulances are parked in front of the building; one looks as though it rammed the back of the one in front of it. No doubt the ambulance driver got a surprise from the "dead" body he was transporting to the morgue.

It appears that everyone in the town rushed to get to the hospital, because the parking lot is full. The doors have been broken out as have most of the windows. There are a few body parts laying around on the lawn and blood splatter on the walls. I doubt anyone in the town made it out alive. All day long we have been sitting in this house, watching and waiting for our chance to head toward the hospital. When we go, it will have to be a very fast trip...we can't take any chances. My arm is killing me, so I will be nearly useless against an attack. If we shoot any guns, it will attract lots of unneeded attention from the undead of the city. I have a paper slicer handle I found in the marketing building; Spook has a wooden flag pole. We both have guns with us, just in case things get really bad.

There are pictures hung on the wall in this house of an old man and his wife. I have been looking at all the pictures around the house; it looks like a nice family once lived here. I think they had either 2 or 3 kids, but I'm not sure. In some photos, there are three kids, but in some there are only two. They were also very clean people. There isn't a single piece of paper laying out anywhere. It looks as if everything is neatly in its place. While going through the house, I found some really nice clothes that looked like they fit me, so I cleaned up really good and changed clothes for the first time in quite a while. It is strange how nice clean clothes feel on your body, when you have gone this long wearing bloody and stained clothes. It was like a shopping spree for us. In a matter of hours, we had gone through every square inch of the house. We took what we thought we could use. Everything else, we left where ever it fell. We laughed, thinking about how upset the old woman would be if she came home and found her house in shambles. I doubt she will ever come home though.

We have decided to make our way to the hospital later this evening, whether it is totally safe or not. If we don't get back soon, Ken may not be alive.

Day 39

Well, we were all set to go yesterday, when out of nowhere we were attacked by three zombies! I don't know how they got in, but Spook heard a noise in the kitchen. We grabbed our makeshift weapons and headed that way. When we got in the kitchen, they quickly turned to look at us. Now I don't think they have any brain function other than to eat, but I could almost swear we startled them. Their dead white eyes got wider, their heads swung to one side, mouths open salivating for dinner. The smell that came from their bodies almost made me vomit. Being dead for over a month, their bodies were also decaying more than I had seen. These three looked like they had been dead...or undead for quite some time. The skin around their wounds had turned black from rot; dried blood covered their faces. These were starving zombies. Their movements were quicker. It seems as if the hungrier they get, the faster they move.

    Before I knew it, they were upon us. Their teeth snapping closed like a dogs. The first one went after Spook. His wooden flagpole came crashing down across the face of the first. Once he hit the ground, the second jumped towards spook. With a somewhat awkward grace, the pointed end of the pole impaled the second zombie under the jaw and up into his head, killing him instantly. Before I could say anything, the third one was after me. I pulled my pipe back, ready for the kill, when a hand grabbed my ankle, knocking me off my feet, my weapon sliding across the floor. When I hit the ground, I was face to face with the first zombie. He flung his head toward mine, desperately trying to pull my face off with his teeth. I moved back just in time, but the third one was swooping down onto me.

    Spook ran up behind the third one, grabbed him by the head and pulled him off me. I reached around for something...anything to bash the first ones head in, but found nothing. I got my feet and ran into the living room, grabbed a very heavy glass lamp and made my way back into the kitchen. When I got there, Spook at finished off the second undead bastard and was moving to take out the first one, who was now on his feet again. Together, we walked right up to him. The vacant look in his eyes showed no fear, no hate, and no sadness. He did not know what his fate was about to become, he just knew of the hunger. I hit him in the head with the lamp hard enough to damn near decapitate him.

After the fight, we were too tired to attempt a trip to the hospital. We have barricaded all the doors and windows and will rest the remainder of the evening.

Tomorrow, barring another attack, we will head that way.

Day 40

We made it to the hospital.

Before we left, we both covered ourselves in the blood of the dead zombies, to cover our scent. When we left the house, we slowly made our way toward the building. We kept our selves hidden as much as possible. Once we got inside, we quickly made our way into medical supply room. We packed as much as we could into a bag we had found inside the house. The trip was going much better than either of us had thought. Not even a single zombie glanced in our direction the entire way to the building, nor once inside. Things were going so good, too good. We knew it wouldn't be long before we were noticed. In and out in less than ten minutes. That was our goal and that's what we stuck to. Right at the ten minute mark, we were stepping out the front doors. Five minutes after that, we were back in the street, making our way to the house, when the zombie blood smell wore off. Spook said he thought it was our sweating that caused the odor to attract them; they were on to us. We began to run. As we began running, I glanced back behind me to see about 50 of the undead monsters coming after us. I am not totally sure, but I would swear they were almost trying to run after us! We easily got away, but I know they are getting faster! This scares the hell out of me.

We are hidden in an old train station. There doesn't seem to be anyone around, so I think we are going to try to get some rest and make our way back to the marketing building first thing in the morning. Tonight we are going to sleep in shifts. Spook said he is wired from the action, so he will take the first shift. Two hours is better than nothing right!?

Day 41

We got plenty of sleep last night and headed back to the office first thing this morning. We arrived to find the place empty! The door had been broken down and blood covered the floor. No one was around, not even a zombie. The only hint we got to their whereabouts was a letter written on the wall. The note read "attacked, leaving. If safe, stay there". So this is where we have been sitting all day. We have barricaded the door once again and have a nice open view of the road from the 2nd floor. Not much has been going on today, so this is going to be a short update.

The only news I have to share is that Spook seems to not be feeling well. He was looking a little pale this morning and throughout the day. He says he is feeling fine, but I can see sweat beading up and when he doesn't think I am watching, I see him shiver a little. I'm not trying to jump to conclusions, but I am afraid he may have been bitten while in the old couple's house. That was the only time we have left each others side. I am planning on keeping a close eye on him.

Day 42

    Spook is sick. He is very sick. All night last night and all day today he has been throwing up and moaning in pain. There is no doubt he is infected and going through "the change". I haven't got the heart to ask him when he was bitten; not that I think he would admit to it even if he had been. I have quarantined him in a back supply closet. I told him it is for his protection "in case they attack while he is sick". I know he is not buying that excuse though. I am unsure as to what to do about him. I know he will be one of *them* within the next few hours or days, but he has been a great friend and protector. If I wait until he has fully changed, I will have to fight him to kill him, unless I watch him every second of the day, and kill him in that brief moment just before he reawakens as one of the living dead. Hell, I could go ahead and end his life now, but I just don't have the heart.

    I am glad Paula is not here to see this. I am glad that psycho Malice isn't around either, he would have blown Spooks head off at the first sign. Cole and Tonya don't need to see this either...they have been through too much already....and Ken....Oh God, I wonder if he is even still alive.

    I haven't had the time to think about what could have happened to the others. Whose blood is all over the place? Who is alive and who is dead? What if they are facing the same dilemma? What would they do? What would anyone do?

    Ok, I think if I just watch him closely, I should be able to kill him before he is able to complete the change and kill me. But how should I do this? Shooting a gun will be much too loud and will attract the attention of all the zombies within about 100 miles. I could grab some sort of blunt object laying around...maybe like a fax machine or a cash register.....no, those are too heavy and bulky. I don't know that I would be able to overpower him, he is a big guy, and so snapping his neck ninja style is also out. (Not that I could snap some ones neck ninja style, but I need more ideas). I hate even thinking about this. Spook has been a great ally to me.

    Another thing I have been thinking about today is what happens when Spook is gone? If the others return (and that is a huge if!), If Ken is gone, that will leave me with a widow, a pissed off lesbian out for revenge, and a teenager not even old enough to drive. Things aren't looking real good right now I have no idea how to get out of this one or even what to do once we are out of this mess. If the others don't return soon, I will have to begin making my way back towards my house and back to Darcy, though every day, I am getting less and less optimistic about her survival. Spook has gotten very quiet in the room. Maybe he is asleep, or maybe...

Day 43

Spook is a zombie. I tried to get in the supply room in time to kill him right before he changed, but I was too late.

When I opened the door, Spook was sitting, with his hands in his lap, face looking down. He was not breathing or moving. I thought for a minute that maybe he had just gotten really sick and died from his illness. He looked like he was sleeping. Without warning, he flung his head up, looking directly at me. I jumped about 10 feet back, tripping and falling over a bucket that had been lying in the floor. As I slid backwards, spook jumped on top of me. His once brown eyes were stone white. The blood that once flowed through his body had stopped moving and was creating a purple look to his face. His movements were deliberate and quick. He wanted nothing in this world other than to pick my bones clean. Spooks weight was overwhelming to me. I was fighting just to keep his mouth away from my body. I had my left hand under his chin, raising his face up in the air. With my right hand, I felt around for something...anything! I felt my hand wrap around something hard and round like a broom, or a mop handle. All I could do is swing towards his face. I could hear the wood slam against the side of his head, but he did not even flinch. He was beginning to overpower me. My muscles, still weak from the accident and previous fights were slowly giving out. I swung again and again at his head, each time, the wood would break and splinter, but he would not even acknowledge that he had been hit. As my arm began to collapse, my whole body gave out; I could no longer fight him off. I had felt bad about killing him while he was still alive, even though I knew this could happen. My delaying would be my demise. I begged God to take me back in time just one hour before. I would have bashed his brains into a bloody mush without hesitation. My wish was never granted. I gave up. I could fight him off no longer. As I dropped my hand, his teeth came roaring towards my face. All I remember seeing is his teeth, then a bright flash of metal. I passed out from exhaustion and stress.

When I awoke, Malice was standing over top of me. He was studying my face and arms; no doubt looking for bite marks. He had this scared/ wounded dog look on his face. Before I could say anything, he helped me up, asked if I was ok and turned toward the door. I asked where he was going, to which he replied "I have a woman back home waiting for me. I'm going to her". I didn't try to stop him, but he had now saved my life a few times, so for that I am grateful. As he walked out the door, I stayed lying on the counter, where he put me. I stared up at the ceiling for a long time, listening to Spook crash around in the supply closet.

I have some hard decisions to make now. If I stay here, Spook will eventually get out of the closet and the zombies will eventually get in here. If I leave, I may never see the others again. I just want to be home. I want to be sitting on my couch at my house, flipping through my TV, complaining about nothing being on.

The world has changed, nothing will ever be the same again. I am stuck in a small town somewhere far away from where I need to be, surrounded by the living dead. I can't help but laugh.

And cry.

Day 44

I am not too sure where to go or what to do. All I laid awake all night last night listening to Spook banging and crashing around in the back room. He moans just like the rest of them. I don't know what to do with him. I guess I could just leave him in there until he starves to death, if that would ever happen. What if Paula does come back, what then? I just don't know if I can take that chance. I have decided to leave tomorrow, with or without anyone. I am going to write on the walls, just in case they do come back, so they will know where I went and not to open the storage room door.

I have been watching the zombies as they walk down the road searching for food. I am sure they are getting faster. Maybe they are just getting hungrier. The human population has to be dwindling down by now. I wonder how many of us are left. I am sure there has to be quite a few others...maybe they got to some safety before all hell broke loose. There is an Air Force base just down the road from my house. I wonder how many people made it into the nuclear fallout shelter. God, if even one of them were infected, the whole shelter would be dead by now. At any rate, I am going to have to be more careful when I pack up and leave. I believe the best route will be finding a truck or some other large vehicle. I can out run them, but since they don't breathe, they won't get tired. I wonder how fast they will get. Right now, they are moving at about a normal walking speed. I have no idea what I will do if they begin to run. I am going to attempt to rest a little before I start packing. I am going to lock myself in a closet down the hall for a little bit. If I am going to do this alone again, I need my rest. Good night.

Day 45

A Reunion.

Well, sometimes good things can happen at the worst of times. Early this morning, I was sleeping (longer than I had anticipated) in the closet, when I was awoken by a noise. I heard things crashing around in the room just beyond the door. I jumped up, grabbed a metal curtain rod I found in the closet, and slowly opened the door. I had decided to just come out swinging, but when I opened the door, I saw Tonya standing directly in front of me; her hand reaching out to the door knob. We both jumped back just a little. When we finally realized who each other was, we hugged. I glanced around to see who all had made it. I saw Cole and Ken, but no Paula. I began to ask where she was, when Tonya began to cry. It took a minute to figure out what had upset her so bad. Paula wasn't there, because Paula had not survived the attack that sent them running. Apparently, while Spook and I were gone, the others were hanging around, watching for any sign of us to return. Paula was positioned on the second floor, looking out the window, when she came running down the stairs, happy we had returned. She flung the door open, to meet us with open arms. What she found on the other side though, was two zombies looking for their evening meal. Tonya said it was very sudden. Paula flung the door open and within seconds, the two zombies were on her. The first bit into her throat, ripping veins and arteries out with every bite. The second went for her arm. Cole said Paula hit the ground, probably died of a heart attack immediately. He said when the zombies realized there were others in the room, they moved quickly towards them. Tonya said they hit one of the zombies in the head with a chair, the other one, they hit with anything they could find. Tonya said Cole helped get Ken out the door, while Tonya quickly wrote a note on the wall, to let me know what had happened. She said they all made it out just as the zombies were getting back up. She told me how they ran about two blocks, until they could not run any longer. Cole said they found a firehouse and ducked inside there, where they have been since. Inside the fire house, they found a little medicine that they used on Kens wounds.

Ken looked a little better than he did the last time I had seen him. He was able to stand up on his own, and could even walk around a little. His wound however, looked really bad. The area directly around it had turned a dark red color and a visible red line ran down his leg from the wound. I could tell he was in some pretty major pain, because he didn't talk much and when he did, he took quick shallow breaths. I gave him some pain pills that Spook and I had found at the hospital; he was all too eager to take them. I know he is dying...he knows he is dying, but we all try to hold on as long as we can.

I told the others about our trip and about what had happened to Spook. Though they didn't agree with me keeping him in the storage room, they said they understood. The one thing we all agreed on though, was that we had to get out of there and we had to get on the road. Sitting around in one place for too long would lead to all of our deaths. W e decided tonight we would head back to the fire station and take one of the smaller fire trucks that were still in the house. From there, we would make our way back to the city. No one wanted to plan any further than that, because no one knew if we would even make it that far. We decided that like an alcoholic, we would take it day by day. Although it has been a somewhat happy day, our happiness has been over shadowed by all the bad things going on around us. Spook is locked in a the storage room directly behind us, Paula is dead and now her body is missing, and Ken is going to die, no matter what we do. We have a long struggle ahead of us. Death is surrounding us, begging for us to join it. Death is taking everyone away. For now, at least we have each other.....if only for a little while longer.

Day 46

We made it to the Firehouse without any issues. We went really slowly the whole way there, mainly for Ken, who could barely walk, but also because we were all exhausted and did not want to run into any zombies along the way. When we got to the firehouse, everything was prepared and ready to go. The others had packed everything we needed for a long trip while they were hiding out there. We wasted no time getting on the road; a lot of bad things had happened in this town and we were all very ready to leave it long behind us. No one had any idea where we were, or how to get to the city, so we pulled out of the firehouse and turned the way we thought it should be. I suggested we find a gas station and grab a map as soon as possible. While driving down the road through the little town, we saw zombies everywhere. They were wandering down the street in no particular direction. They would hear us coming and start walking towards our truck. We began looking like the pied piper....now if only we could find a cliff.

We made one last turn, to head out of town, when we saw Paula; or I guess I should say zombie Paula. She turned just as the others had, staring at us with no comprehension as to who we were. Her eyes had turned that all too familiar dead white. Her neck had been ripped open to the point of near decapitation and her arm from the elbow down to the wrist was nothing but bone. She turned and began coming towards the truck. She did not care who we were, she just wanted us for food.

I slowed the truck down, waiting for her to get a little closer to us. Maybe it wasn't a smart thing to do, because it only allowed the zombies to get closer to us. Tonya was screaming at me to drive....Cole was yelling something about how close they were getting to us, while Ken just stared out the window; the spark of life quickly draining from his eyes. I didn't care what they were saying. I could not allow Paula to go on like this. I felt a thud as a few zombies banged on the back of the truck, desperately looking for a way in. I waited just a few more seconds. I could see the zombies converging on the back of the truck. In front was a group of about 20 or more, heading our way. Tonya now hysterically, screaming, tried to get into the driver's seat to take over. I just shoved her away from me. I was in control of things...I knew what I was doing.

Paula had made her way to the driver's side of the truck now. She was about 20 feet away, when I quickly rolled down the window about half way. I grabbed one of the guns I had laying in the seat next to me and pointed it directly at her head. "Good Bye Paula" I yelled out to her, as I pulled the trigger....nothing happened. I pulled it again...still nothing happened. By this point, the truck was completely surrounded by zombies; even Ken was beginning to look scared. Without thinking, I slammed on the gas, running over four or five of the undead and scattering a dozen more out of the way. I looked in the rear view mirror as I drove away, watching Paula get smaller and smaller.

I am not sure where we are headed, but at least we aren't stuck here anymore. Good Bye Paula and Spook. It was a pleasure knowing you.

Day 47

Just when things look like they are getting good, life has a way of coming back and beating you down just a little to let you know who is really in charge.

Shortly after we left town, we found an old abandoned gas station. Cole ran inside to get a map while Tonya and I doctored up Ken as best we could. After waiting for what seemed like an hour, I heard Cole running back to us. He had a map in one hand and a machete in the other. He had found it behind the counter in the store. As he approached us, he lost his footing on some loose gravel. The map sailed into the wind away from us, but the machete came straight towards Tonya. Instinctively, I flung my hand out to try to stop the blade from slicing her face in two. Unfortunately, the blade sunk deep into the palm of my hand. Blood immediately burst all over us. I grabbed a medical dressing from the back of the fire truck and some antibacterial spray. It was deep, very deep; I could see bone and meat. My main concern was for all of our safety. If even one of the nearby zombies would have caught the scent of my blood, we would have been surrounded once again. I immediately ripped off my shirt and wrapped it around my hand. Once I stopped the bleeding, Tonya stitched me up; yet again, I have stitches. My hand has been hurting all day, but luckily I think it should heal without any problems. I am sure I need a Tetanus shot, but none are available, so I will have to hope for the best.

     We have decided to camp here for the night. I found some pain pills that I plan on loading up on this evening. I am not going to be able to write much more today because of the pain. Hopefully I can get a good night sleep and be prepared for what life throws at us tomorrow.

Day 48

The hand is feeling a little better today. You never realize how important it is, until it is out of commission. I will never take my hand for granted again!

Tonya is driving us now. Cole is in the back as a watch; both for zombies and watching over Ken, who is not doing very well at all. The wound on his leg is turning black and has a very bad odor. He has been sick for a few hours now and has been complaining that his leg is beginning to itch. We are trying to keep him drugged up as much as we can; it is all we can do for him right now.

Moving has been slow. Based on the map, we should be in the city within the next few days. Once in the city, as long as things go right for us, we should be at my house within a week!!! That makes me Very happy. It seems the closer we get, the more cars are blocking the road. I guess when the first wave of undead began, people panicked and tried to get away to anywhere they could. For some, it was to get out of the city; for others, it was going into the city. Earlier we passed by a brand new Lamborghini Murcielago. Cole was half joking around about getting in the car and following us. We all had a good laugh, but I know every one of us would gladly do the same. I bet some really rich guy had the car on order for months. The dealership probably called to tell him it arrived. I bet that rich bastard called all his equally rich friends to brag about his latest purchase; he was probably even throwing himself a party for buying the car. I bet he picked up the car, while the first major attack began. I am sure he thought he could outrun any zombie in that rocket. I guess he never thought about traffic. I can see him now, sitting all smug in his car, honking for the other less fortunate scum of the Earth people to get the hell out of his way. He lays on the horn, rolls down his window to scream at the others to move, when he is pulled out of the car by his head. All his money couldn't keep him safe or alive...but damn, I bet driving that thing would be worth dying for.

    We have stopped at a hotel in a small town that appears to be abandoned. The beds are really big, but hard as a rock. We have decided to all stay in the same room, for safety. We also got a room on the second floor and barricaded the stairs for extra protection. I need to get a little more sleep.
Tomorrow I get closer to being home!

Day 49

    Where do I begin today??? I guess, as they say, at the beginning.

    We all woke up at the same time. It was as if we all knew something bad was going to happen. Almost instantly, we all realized that Ken was gone; not dead, but gone. His stuff was still right where he left it, but he was nowhere to be found. Where the hell could he have gone? When we got to the hotel, he was barely able to walk up the stairs by himself.

    We didn't know what to do. Ken was our friend but we knew he would be dead within a few days anyway. Maybe he wanted to leave us, like a dog that wanders away from his owners' house right before he dies. We were not sure if we should go looking for him or wait for him to come back, or if we should just leave without him.

    Tonya made the decision for us. Before we could say anything, she stormed out the door, running as fast as she could towards the stairway. By the time Cole and I got to the stairs, Tonya had already made her way over the barricade. She was calling out for Ken the whole time she was running. Cole reached her before I did (I'm old, so cut me some slack). He grabbed her by the arm, causing her to fall backwards. When I caught up with them, she had calmed down just a little. She was still frantic to find him, but she was a little more relaxed and ready to form plan as opposed to running onto the battlefield yelling for the enemy to come get you.

    Before we could even start to form a plan, we see Ken driving the same Lamborghini we had passed yesterday!! He pulled up right next to us; the smile on his face shining brighter than the shadow of death hanging over him. Tonya didn't know whether to laugh, cry, or drag Ken out of the car and beat his ass; none of us did. Ken coughed a little, in between laughing. He had tears in his eyes as he told us how and why he got the car.

    Ken woke up early in the morning long before the rest of us. He knew he was never going to get a chance to drive his dream car, unless he took control and went for it. He made his way over the barricades and down to the parking lot. Once he got that far, he began going car to car until he found some keys still in the ignition. He hopped in the car and headed towards his dream. Once he got there, he rammed the other cars out of the way using an old pickup truck parked close by. He didn't care how much noise he made, he just wanted that car. Once there was a big enough path, he walked up to the side of the car. He put his hands on the door, rubbing the paint and day dreaming about a nice long country drive on the twisty mountain roads that he had grown up on. He slowly opened the car door and slid behind the wheel. Turning the key, the car instantly roared to life. Ken drove for miles and miles listening to a "*Code Atom*" cd the previous owner had left in the cd changer. He was living his dream. He decided to drive the car back to us, so we could all have a chance to enjoy it; he wanted us to feel the happiness he felt.

    After a brief scolding from me, I helped Ken out of

the car and slid into it myself. The seat was soft and comfortable. I rolled the windows down, turned up the music and drove as fast as I could down the empty streets, swerving to miss the straggling zombies in the middle of the road. As free as I felt, the knowledge of real life kept me from enjoying myself too much. I drove the car for about ten minutes, and then brought it back for Tonya to drive. She jumped behind the wheel, burning the rubber off both back tires as she slid sideways out of the parking lot. I could just barely hear her squealing with delight as she turned the corner. After about 20 minutes, she returned with the same grin I had just seen on Kens face half an hour ago. Cole talked us in to letting him take it for a spin. No one was happy about it, but we all decided he should be allowed to enjoy the better things in life as well. Ken said he wanted to ride with him just in case anything happened to him. I tried to object, but Tonya agreed that it would be a good idea for Ken to ride along, after all, without him, we wouldn't have this minor luxury. The two of them got in the car and after a brief lesson, Cole mirrored Tonya's exit out of the parking lot.

After what seemed like an hour, we heard the unmistakable sound of metal on metal or in this case, carbon fiber on metal. Tonya and I ran as fast as we could towards the sound. As we turned the corner, we could see the front of the car firmly planted into the side of a Volkswagen Jetta. We were still pretty far away from the wreck, but not too far away to see someone walk from a nearby building. The person walked directly to the passenger side. As we got closer, to our horror, we could see it was a zombie. He had already begun chewing on Kens shoulder before we could get to them. Cole sat in the drivers' seat, unable to get out of the car, thanks to a jammed door. I could hear him screaming and banging on the door, desperately trying to get away. As we approached the car, the zombie looked up and directly at us, Kens fresh blood flowing from his mouth. He ignored us and continued to rip flesh and meat off of Ken's bones. The sound of Ken screeching in pain only lasted for a couple seconds, as his spirit released him from the horror. Tonya grabbed a metal construction zone sign that was lying on the ground. She walked directly up to the back of the feasting zombie and slammed the sign down directly on his back. The zombie barely flinched as he turned to grab her. Before he could even raise his hand toward her, she used the sign as an ax, swinging it by the corner; she completely decapitated the undead monster. His lifeless body hit the ground spewing blood like a fountain. Tony reached in to help Cole out of the drivers' seat. Because the driver's door was jammed, He would have to exit out the passenger's side. Just as Cole's foot crossed over Kens lap, a newly animated hand reached up, grabbing his shoe, causing him to fall face first to the ground. Tonya desperately pulled on Cole's arms, trying to pry him away from this new monster. Cole was kicking Ken in the face, also trying anything he could to get away. I ran to the driver's side of the car, pulled out a pistol from my belt, and pointed the gun at Kens head. Without saying any witty remark, or a cool catch phrase like what you see in the movies, I pulled the trigger. Kens grip instantly released Cole's foot, as chunks of his scalp sprayed the interior of the car.

    We ran as fast as we could back to the hotel. The gun shot was loud enough to attract a lot of attention. By the time we reached the hotel, we could see dozens of the undead making their way towards us. We immediately jumped into the fire truck and sped down the road, leaving this town long behind us.
We have decided to sleep in the truck tonight. We are parked directly on the interstate with a group of other cars. I think we will be safe for the night. We fit in pretty good here, so we shouldn't attract any attention. No one wants to talk about what happened to our friend. We just sit in silence each remembering him in our own way.

Day 50

    We awoke with the sun today, though I don't think anyone slept very good last night. I know I woke up quite a few times in the night, hearing the sounds of the living dead right outside the truck. I would hear a moan or a bang on the side of the truck, then silence. If anyone else was awake, they never said anything.

When we got up this morning, I decided to take over the driving duties. Normally, driving for long distances is pretty easy, but when you have to swerve around cars and avoid large groups of zombies standing in the road, driving becomes hard work. I believe today we should be back at my work exit. If we get there in enough time, maybe we can stop for the night.

While driving, I was surprised to see a car quickly coming up behind us. The car flew around cars as if they weren't there. The car was moving so fast that within seconds of noticing it, it was already on our bumper. The driver began honking the horn and flashing his lights at us. I decided to pull over and let him pass. As I slowed down and pulled over, the driver passed us. While he passed, he held out his left hand and flipped us off! I was prepared to let it go, but Cole yelled out the window "go fuck yourself" to the driver. When the car pulled in front of us, he slammed on the brakes, causing us to have to lock down our brakes in order to keep from hitting him.

After waiting for about a minute, both the driver side and the passenger's side doors opened. Two men stepped out of the car. The driver was about my size, wearing a Gators college football hat and a shirt that read "Shiki is the new Black" (whatever that means); Out of the passenger's side, a big guy wearing a T-shirt that read "I Wanna Party With You" stepped out carrying a shotgun over his shoulder. The driver began screaming at us for being bad drivers and said something about watching our mouths. Tonya, Cole, and I all got out of the truck; each of us carrying a gun. Both of the men came over to where I was standing and just stared at me for a minute. The big guy with the "I Wanna Party With You" shirt looked around, but his eyes landed on Tonya. He walked over to her slowly, like a drunk guy in a bar, walking up to a really hot girl that he has no chance with.

    I asked the driver what his problem was and why he was in such a hurry. The driver just continued to yell at me for going "too slow". As he screamed louder and louder, I glanced over in Tonya's direction to see what was happening on her end. The passenger was leaning over her, trying to press his body against hers. Before I could say anything, Tonya pulled her gun out and pressed the barrel into the big guy's nose. At that exact moment, the driver pulled a pistol out and pointed it directly at me. Cole, who was standing back at the truck, grabbed his own gun and pointed it at both of the men, moving between the two back and forth, unsure as to who he should aim at.

    There we stood, guns pointed at each other, ready to shoot each other without hesitation, when out of the woods beside us, came a group of zombies. Without thinking, we all turned our guns on them. They quickly moved in our direction. As the first one's foot hit the pavement, the driver began shooting. We continued to shoot until they were all gone. As the last one hit the ground, all guns went back to their original location; pointed at each other. The driver began to laugh. Pretty soon, we were all laughing. We had just played out a scene that could be in a movie. The driver lowered his gun and held out his hand to shake mine. He introduced himself as Dustin, and then introduced his passenger as Roger. They were heading to the city to "take advantage of the luxuries it had to offer". They had been driving for hours and wanted to be downtown by night fall. Roger told us he was from Mexico and had met Dustin in Florida just before the uprising had begun. He said they were both on vacation and at the same hotel when everything happened. Dustin said he and his wife were visiting some friends when it all went down. He said he woke up one night to find his wife missing. He said all her things were where she had left them, but she was gone. He said Roger located her body in another room of the hotel. From then on, they decided to stay close and help each other.

     We told them we were making our way into the city and asked if they wanted to join with us. After a few minutes of them talking and debating, they agreed to follow us, just to the city.

     Tonya didn't trust either of them, especially Roger. She said he gave her a very strange feeling. To tell the truth, he gave me the same feeling. If it wasn't for my desire to keep as many people around me as possible, I would have wished them luck and waved them good bye.

I hope I haven't made a bad decision.

Day 51

Back where I started.

51 days ago, I was sitting in the same room I am now. So much has happened in 51 days. This place looks and smells strange.

When we got here late last night, there were no zombies to be seen. We made our way inside and blocked the front door with two desks. With no one (or nothing) getting in or out, we searched the entire building for any of the undead. As I walked toward the break room, I passed the room where I put a fishbowl through my managers' head; her body still lying in the same place I left it, only now, her body had begun decomposing quite badly. After 51 days, the smells coming from that office were overwhelming. I closed the door and moved on. In the break room, I gathered a little bit of food that was still in good condition and a few cans of Coke. We all met back in the "secure" area where I first began this journal. The room was trashed beyond belief. My desk was flipped over, computer lying on the floor, with the monitor smashed in. All the files I spent weeks filing were spread across the floor as well. There was a fair amount of dried blood on the walls and floor. It looks like someone had been in here since I had left. If they were though, they are gone now.

  Feeling safe, we all took a seat to rest and formulate a plan. I made my way to my nice leather chair that I had at one time complained about because the wheels squeaked too much. It's kind of funny how minuscule that problem seems now compared to everything else going on. I remember being so angry that Amanda refused to do anything about it. Now though, it feels like the most comfortable thing I have ever sat in. Tonya and Cole flipped my desk back over and sat on it, while Roger and Dustin both found chairs of their own to sit on.

  I handed everyone a Coke and a small snack size bag of chips. I told my story of how it my journey began and how I ended up here, with Tonya and Cole. Dustin smiled and shook his head at the "adventures" (as he liked to call them) I had. After I had told my story, Tonya and Cole both told theirs. Again, Dustin seemed very interested and even sad at times about the whole ordeal. Roger seemed bored and uninterested in anything any of us had to say. Once all the stories had been told, we were all very sleepy and decided to try and get some rest before we headed out. Our original plan was to have one person stay up as a watch for the rest of us, but we all ended up falling asleep around the same time.

  Sometime around 4 or 5 in the morning, I awoke to

see Roger standing over Tonya. He was staring at her, watching her sleep. I could hear him whispering something to himself has he looked at her. His whispering got louder and it sounded as if he were angry at her. I quickly sat up and asked him what the hell he was doing. Startled, he spun around and looked directly at me. His eyes were opened wide and he was sweating profusely. He yelled at me to "mind my own fucking business", then stomped off to the far corner of the room. His yelling woke up the entire room. Tonya looked freaked out, Cole looked confused and Dustin was pissed off. Roger refused to talk to anyone and has not moved from the corner all morning. Needless to say, no one slept after that.

    We are going to approach Roger in a few minutes, just to see what was going on. Dustin thinks it was just a misunderstanding, Tonya, Cole, and I do not. Misunderstanding or not, I will not allow anyone to make the ones I care about feel uncomfortable. I have a very bad feeling about this guy and do not look forward to what lies ahead for us today.

Day 52

    We approached Roger yesterday evening about his actions the night before. He denied doing anything wrong and even said he had a problem with sleepwalking. What could we say to that?? The subject was dropped after a few threats were issued and he said he completely understood our concerns. I still don't trust him though. I am going to watch him very closely.

So we packed up everything we had and left my old job location. Once we were loaded up, we headed down the path towards my home.

Nothing exciting has been going on today, other than driving very, very slowly. Every couple miles, we have to pull over on the side of the road to get around the abandoned cars, or to siphon gas out of them. The closer we get to the city, the harder it is to drive. I am sure it is only a matter of a few hours before we will have to walk. I am dreading this more than anything else right now. At least we are somewhat safe in our little tank of a vehicle, for now. When we get out walking, I am not going to be much help if things get bad, because of the stitches in my hand and arm. Then there is the whole Roger issue. I have to watch out for the zombies and now this crazy guy. I just hope I can protect everyone.

We are stopping for more gas and to discuss our route. It is very eerie how quiet it has gotten. No sounds of cars or airplanes, no sounds of children playing, or construction sites; even the birds are silent. The sky has been a light gray color the past few days, though it hasn't rained in weeks. I am not sure what is going on with the world around us, but whatever it is, it can't be good.

Day 53

One last drunk.

Yesterday, we decided to stop at a hotel right before we went on into the city. We had abandoned the vehicles about two hours after I had finished writing in the journal, so we were exhausted by the time we got to the hotel. We decided to stay in the same room again, though I wasn't very happy with that decision, because of the Roger situation. In the end, we decided it was safer to stay together; though safer for whom, I am still trying to figure that out.

Once we were settled in the room, we decided to have a look around the hotel, just to make sure there were no zombies running around. We made our way into the lobby, where behind the counter; there was the nicely rotting corpse of a little old lady. She looked to be in her 70's, though because of the rotting of her flesh, it was hard to tell. She sat on a tall wooded chair; her head facing down to the ground, as if she was looking at her feet. Tonya went in for a closer look. As she approached, she yelled out to us "Hey, her name is Fran, isn't that so sweet?" Just as the word sweet passed over her lips, Fran sat straight up in the chair, looked directly at Tonya, and then lunged for her. Just inches before Fran's mouth would have made contact with Tonya's neck, Cole slammed a chair over the old zombie's head. Once on the ground, he took a piece of the now busted up chair and drove it through her eye socket. We all could do nothing but laugh.....we laughed! What the hell is wrong with us??

After the lobby area, we all wanted nothing more than to check out the bar. Once we got there, there were hundreds of bottles of alcohol. Anything and everything you could imagine was behind that bar. We proceeded to try everything. I don't have many details about what happened after that, because I don't remember. All I remember is shots of Jagermiester and Dustin getting naked...

When we woke up this morning, Roger and Tonya were gone.

We are leaving right now to go find her. I swear to God, if he has hurt one hair on her body, I will chop him into tiny pieces myself. We are all just hoping they got drunk and passed out somewhere.
Either way, I am never drinking again.

Day 54

Tonya and Roger are nowhere to be found. We have gone room to room, searching the entire area, but have found nothing. Dustin thinks they have been eaten or turned, but the rest of us think otherwise. We are going to continue to look everywhere in this town that we can. I am determined to find them both, dead, alive, or living dead, I have to know what happened to them. There have not been many zombies in this area that we have seen, so we feel pretty safe.

Earlier this morning, we did stumble across two zombies. They had long dreadlocks and wore tie-dyed shirts. They were covered in dried blood from head to toe. One was a girl with a blue bandanna on; she was chewing on a severed hand. The other was a man with a "Rasta" hat on his head; he was eating a severed foot. When they saw us coming, they both jumped to their feet and headed straight towards us. Now, I wouldn't call it a run, but I know for a fact, they were moving quite fast. With all of us ready for them, they went down quickly. The girl hit the ground hard and as she started to get up, I smashed her head in with a large rock I had found. Dustin and Cole took care of the guy. Other than those two, we haven't seen any others.

We are headed off to go look some more. I am really going into full on panic mode. Tonya means so much to me.

She has been a very close friend through all this. I will do whatever I can to find her, no matter what it takes.

Day 55

I wish I had more to write about today, but it has been a very uneventful day. We spent all day looking for Tonya and Roger. All we found today was a pair of Tonya's shoes. They were lying on the ground by an old office complex. We didn't see any zombies today. I wish I could say that today was a good day, but without Tonya, it is just another day. We need her here with us. We are determined to not give up on her. I will not give up on her. We are going to search some of the local areas some more tonight. I will post more as soon as I get more information.

Day 56

We have searched for Tonya pretty much nonstop for the past few days and have no leads to follow. I have no idea as to what to do or where to go from here. Cole has said he is not going anywhere until she is found...dead or alive, so it looks like we will be continuing to look. I have been in every building within about a 3 mile radius, and have only run into less than 5 zombies. I am hoping the zombies have begun starving to death or rotting away; that would make things so much easier. After running into the "Rasta" zombies, we decided it would be easier to stay hidden and not fight.

As we wondered through the town, we came across store after store that had been looted, trashed, and even burned. It looked like the people panicked and began destroying the town, like so many people have done in the past. Looking at this town though, I can only imagine what the big city will look like when we get there. From where we are right now, I can see the cityscape in the distance; it looks like it always has, almost as if nothing had happened. Sadly, we know better.

We have one more place to look tomorrow, and then we will have covered the entire city. It is likely he got a car and got out of the city. I am going to bring up to the others tomorrow that maybe we should go ahead and head toward the city. More than likely he would have headed straight into the city. It is very large, with lots of places to hide. Once the town has been gone over with a fine tooth comb, we have nowhere else to look. My biggest fear is that he took her in the opposite direction (if Roger even took her). We just don't know what happened to them.
Things have been quiet for a few days now; I hope they stay that way.

Day 57

It is so late right now and I am so very tired. We decided to leave the town this morning. We haven't (nor will we) give up on Tonya, but there is nothing for us left here. We have searched everywhere we can imagine to no avail. We drove for as long as we possibly could, until the roads became too heavily blocked with parked and abandoned cars. We were still a good 15 miles away from the big city, but there was no way for us to get around the other vehicles. We walked for almost five miles total this afternoon and this evening. We only encountered one or two zombies along the way. I'm not sure what's going on; I don't know where they have all gone, or are going. I am hoping they have all died for good this time.

I really have nothing to write about again today; all we did was walk. It is now 2 o'clock in the morning; I need some sleep if we are going to be walking again tomorrow.

Day 58

After walking all day today, we stopped at a hotel right on the outside of an amusement park. From the room, you can see the rides that months ago would fling people into the air, or have them spin around in circles until they got sick; today, those same rides are skeletons; old reminders of what life was like before the dead began to rise. The hotel we stopped at is a very swanky hotel that 58 days ago, I would not have been able to afford; now I am in the biggest, nicest suite they have. This room has around 1800 square feet of living space and a balcony that stretches the length of the room, and faces the amusement park. On the inside, the room has hard wood floor throughout, except for imported Spanish tile in the bathrooms and kitchen. There are four room; two master suites with a king size bed and hot tub. The other two rooms both have two queen size beds and Xbox 360's hooked up to 35 inch flat screen HDTV's.

The room is located on the 7th floor of the resort. We stopped the elevators and blocked the stairwell, so no unwanted "intruders" can get to us. Earlier, we stood on the balcony and watched one or two zombies make their way towards the amusement park. They would wander around, never focusing on anything, just kind of "there" with no place to go. Every now and then, one of them would get a whiff of us, then turn and look directly at us. I am not sure how many there may be, but I do know that at least four have made their way into the hotel after us.

Cole has been sitting in the living room all afternoon, pacing the floor, trying to think of ways to find Tonya and I am sure, what to do once we find her. I have no doubt she is long gone. I just don't have the heart to tell Cole. Dustin refuses to even think that Roger would have done anything

to hurt Tonya. I still don't know what to think.
Tomorrow we are planning on setting up a watch on the balcony most of the day; hopefully, we will be able to see something that will help lead us to Tonya or safety.

Day 59

We have been sitting on the balcony for hours and have seen nothing new or out of the ordinary. Dustin and Cole have both been taking turns throwing plates and silverware at zombies that have been passing by below us. We all had a good laugh at a fork that got stuck in one zombie's cheek. Cole yelled till the zombie looked up at us, then he dropped it straight down. The fork went straight into it's cheek, like a knife going through butter. Cole jumped up and down cheering for himself and yelled "extra points! I get extra points for it sticking". I guess they have their own point system that I have not been able to figure out.

I am not sure how many of the undead there are in the hotel now, but if I had to guess, I would say somewhere around 10 - 15. For some reason I haven't been worried about it. I guess it's because I am comfortable here and feel very safe. The only problem we have right now is lack of food. I am starting to become concerned about that little problem. Sure, we can invade the snack machine down the hall, but that will eventually run out. We have been through worse and I am betting we will go through even harder times soon enough. Darcy always told me to only worry about the things I can control, so that is exactly what I will do.

Cole said he just saw Tonya running away from someone (or something) down in the theme park! Crap! Now we have to find some way to get her.

Day 60

We have all seen Tonya alive now. She is in another building across a pond from us. We have no way of contacting each other, so we don't know what has happened. We are working on a plan to go get her, but I know there are quite a few zombies in the hotel, so any rescue attempt will be very difficult.

After quite a bit of debating, it was decided that I would be the one to go get Tonya in the morning. I have known her longer than Dustin and I just can't trust Cole to stay alive long enough to save her. For some reason, Dustin very much wants to go. I don't know if he just really wants to help, or if he has an ulterior motive. Either way, I don't quite trust him enough; after all, he is the one who brought Roger into our group.

Well, I am going to go ahead and get to bed tonight, I have a very long day ahead of me tomorrow and need to get as much sleep as possible. I don't plan on taking the laptop with me, I am going to just bring what I need to survive and some medical supplies for Tonya, just in case she is injured. As long as everything goes good, I should be back on here tomorrow evening with an update. Wish me luck on my mission, God knows I am really going to need it!

Day 61

Dustin left before I got out of bed yesterday. When I woke up, I went to grab my bag, but it was gone. I ran into Cole's room, where I found him sleeping. When I ran into Dustin's room, he was not there. On his bed was a note. The only words on the note were "I cannot let you go out there. I have gone. Wait for me. I will be back."

Once I got over the first wave of anger, a slight sense of relief passed over me. I have been the one to always go after the hurt and wounded. I was the one that went to find Cole and then went to find medical supplies. Maybe Dustin was right to do this. But I could have gone; my hand is 100% healed as was my shoulder. For the most part, I was healthy and getting really fit, thanks to the diet and exercise I have gotten...(I guess I could call this The Zombie Fit Diet; if the world hadn't gone to shit, I could have marketed this and made billions.)

    Once I read the letter, I ran to the balcony and scanned the grounds around us, looking for any signs of Dustin or Tonya. There is no telling how long he had been gone, so I wasn't sure as to where to look. I ran in and woke up Cole. After I explained what had happened, he joined me on the balcony to help look. After about an hour of scanning the grounds, Cole Yelled "I see them, I see them!" He was pointing to a building directly in front of ours. I wasn't sure, but I could have sworn that I had seen three people. I could definitely make out Tonya and Dustin, but the third person, I couldn't see. I could not see them, until he walked out in to the light. The third person was Roger.

    Something was wrong though. Roger was tied up; his hands were behind his body, feet tied together, just far enough apart so that he could walk, but not run. Across his face were rows and rows of duck tape and a shotgun attached so that the barrel was facing the back of his head. I could not make out what had happened, but I could see Dustin holding the handle of the shotgun and Tonya quickly following behind them both. We watched as they all three made their way into our hotel, careful to avoid any zombies. Before I could even get to the hotel door, I heard the elevator ding, indicating that it had arrived on the floor. I peeked out just enough to see them step off the elevator and head towards us. Dustin told Tonya to block the elevator and double check the doors leading to the stairs. He and his prisoner made their way inside and Tonya soon followed. Once in the room, Tonya ran to Cole and me and hugged us for what seemed like hours. I could tell she had been crying because of the heavy red bags under her eyes and her wrists were black and blue and raw, where it appeared she had been tied up. I wanted to ask what had happened...I wanted to know why Roger was now a prisoner; I wanted to know it all. I asked about a million questions, but they were all exhausted. No one wanted to talk yet, so I didn't push the subject. I can piece together what happened in my mind. On my final question, all Dustin would say was "Tomorrow".

Day 62

    I could hardly sleep last night. I had to know the story. I don't think Dustin slept at all. When I would wake up, I could hear Dustin in the sitting room, pacing back and forth in front of Roger; he was cursing under his breath. Roger looked frightened. Tonya and Cole slept like babies all through the night.

    When everyone got up, we all met in the sitting room. Roger was down on his knees. His face was bruised and bloody. Dustin stood over him with a metal curtain rod. We all sat on the couch in front of them both. Tonya began to speak, but before she could say two words, Dustin grabbed Roger by the back of the head, pulled his face up so they were looking directly face to face. Dustin shouted "I am going to show you more pain than you could ever imagine. You killed my wife; you tried to kill Tonya, now I will kill you myself." The room seemed to drop 20 degrees. We all just stared at them both. I couldn't believe what I was hearing. Before I could protest, Tonya turned to me and nodded her head..."it is true what he is telling us", Tonya almost whispered. "The night we were drinking, I passed out and when I awoke, I was in the trunk of a car", Tonya began. She told her story about how Roger took her to the amusement park and tied her up. She said he would walk around naked, talking to himself repeatedly and even talking about Dustin's wife. She said she fought him off as much as she could, until one day she just "gave in". She told Roger she would do whatever he wanted, as long as he didn't kill her. She said Roger quickly untied her and began stripping her clothes off of her until she was standing in just her panties. As Roger lowered his head to remove her panties, Tonya hit him as hard as she could on the back of his head/neck area. Once he was down, she told how she found a knife Roger had been carrying. She tied him up and left him in the room, with all the doors and windows open. She said she had hoped zombies would have come in and ripped him into pieces. Right as Tonya finished her sentence, Dustin slammed the metal pole across Roger's inner thigh. Roger screamed in agony. Cole began to cry a little. Tonya said she moved from hotel to hotel trying to cover her tracks, but Roger had somehow escaped and found her. She had locked herself in a room, which is when we saw her.

Dustin interrupted her story at this point and began to tell how he had arrived at Tonya's hotel room to see Roger banging on the door. He was foaming at the mouth he was so angry, desperately trying to get in the room. He said he overheard Roger telling Tonya through the door that he would butcher her just as he had done many other women before her. Dustin snuck up behind Roger and knocked him out. He and Tonya together found the duck tape and tied him up, making sure to place the shotgun in a place where all he would have to do is pull the trigger if Roger got out of hand. Tonya said she convinced Dustin to bring Roger back here, instead of killing him right there. She said everyone deserved a "fair trial".

We removed the tape from Roger's mouth. He was drooling and had a large amount of blood flowing over his lips. He begged for forgiveness and even said that Tonya was lying; that she was the one that kidnapped him. He denied killing Dustin's wife in Florida. We didn't buy his story.

I asked Cole and Tonya to leave the room. Once they were gone, I asked Roger to look at me. As his eyes locked on to mine, I could see the guilt and remorse...though I am sure it was only because he had been caught. "I am going to let Dustin do what he sees fit. You have hurt a lot of people, one of which I have grown to love....you deserve no mercy, though I will agree with whatever Dustin decides", I said to Roger. He began to cry and beg for his life. I nodded to Dustin and walked toward the door. I asked Tonya and Cole to go into another room down the hall, then closed and locked the door, sealing Roger's fate.

I am not sure what I should write about what took place next. I could go into graphic details, though I am not sure I even want to remember what I witnessed in that room. Dustin got the vengeance he so desperately needed for his wife. Roger did not die quickly, he died in excruciating pain. His pain ended only when, after knocking out all Rogers teeth with the metal bar, Dustin placed the shotgun into his gaping bloody mouth and pulled the trigger....repeatedly.

We left his body lying on the floor and moved to a new floor in the hotel. We have not spoken about what happened. That chapter is closed for good. Tomorrow we head towards the city.

Day 63

After the past few days' worth of excitement, I am happy to report that nothing out of the ordinary has happened so far today. We were going to go ahead and head a little closer to the city, but have decided to sit back and do a little planning. Tonya and Dustin could also use a little break. I have determined that the easiest way is to go straight through the amusement park. I am a little worried about this, because they have always given me the creeps. Our first step will have to be getting out of the hotel without being seen. Dustin says he knows a way that will keep us undetected. He said it was the way he went when he went after Tonya. I just hope he is correct.

Day 64

We got up early this morning, so we could make our way through the park and get it over with as soon as possible. We took Dustin's route; which as he said, was zombie free. Once we reached the door leading out, we ran as fast as we could across the lawn until we came to the entrance of the park. The front gates had been torn down; I don't know if that means people were trying to get in or out, either way, we all got a little more prepared for what we could face ahead.

We walked through the ticketing booths and through the turnstiles. As we walked through, there were giant cartoon characters staring at us, with larger than life smiles spread across their face. Their hands up, waving at us, inviting us in....or were they daring us to enter?

A happy cartoon song played over the loudspeakers throughout the entire park, leading to the eeriness of the experience. I remember as a kid, walking those same streets with my parents. I remember being so excited to see those characters smiling and hearing that song play in the back ground as I ate my cotton candy and waited in the eternal line for 45 minutes to ride a 2 minute "thrill" ride that would always make me sick. I remember the people dressed in the mouse and cat costumes that used to sign autographs as if they were the actual cartoon characters I watched so intently on the TV. All the happy kids and exhausted parents are now long gone, replaced with piles of trash and other debris blowing around in front of us.

We made our way past the Ferris wheel and spinning rides and were on our way to the big steel coaster that had just opened earlier this year. Darcy and I had been planning on coming out here to ride this big beast sometime before the end of the year. One of the cars could be seen halfway up the large incline. It looked like a couple people were sitting inside, however, their heads were slouched back and you could clearly see one of passengers was missing their arms.

As we passed the giant coaster, we were passing a building that housed a little kiddies' ride. Every amusement park has this kind of ride. You ride on a boat through different "lands" while animatronics kids sing a cute song in their native language. When we got directly in front of the building, a group of about eight zombies walked around the corner. We decided (without saying a word), that we would all run inside the building to get away. We ran through the doors and deep into the building. A long line of boats were parked in the water, guiding us through the maze of rooms. The animatronics kids were standing frozen in the pose they were last in when the power went out at this building. We bobbed and weaved through the rooms and over the boats, steadily making our way to the exit. As we turned one corner, the power to the entire area flashed on. The electronic children all burst to life singing their happy little songs and dancing their happy little dances. The sudden noise was enough to startle us all. Cole jumped back, lost his balance and fell directly into the water. We all turned to help him; no one noticing the zombie that had made his way into the room with us. Just as we pulled Cole out of the water, Dustin turned in time to be face to face with the undead man. The zombies' mouth came snapping down towards Dustin's face. Out of instinct, Dustin leaned way back to avoid the bite, but in doing so, he also fell into the water, bringing a zombie right down on top of him. Blood began bubbling up from under the water. We all stood back, not sure what to do. Cole scrambled out of the water as if he were in a bed of snakes. After what seemed like hours, Dustin came rising out of the bloody water and the zombie came floating to the top. The zombies' body rolled over to reveal a deep gash in his forehead, presumably from hitting his head on the tracks below the water. As we pulled Dustin from the water, the zombie sprung to life, his body twitching and writhing in the water, but unable to stand. We stood and watched him for a few minutes; Tonya began to laugh, soon we all began laughing at him. He looked as though he was having a seizer, but he was fully coherent or as coherent as a zombie can be. He stared up at us, blood flowing from his skull, looking like he would tear us limb from limb if he could; and he would!

We began walking away from the flailing zombie, when we heard a noise behind us. We all turned to see at least twenty zombies, walking through the water straight towards us. Without thinking, I grabbed one of the robot kids, raised it above my head; it's electrical cords hanging down, sparking it's electrical bolts, and awaiting for me to throw it in the water. The zombies began moving faster towards us, their mouths snapping in anticipation. I walked beside the water. I imagined myself in a movie, everything went to slow motion. My eyes on the water, head tilted down; slowly I brought my eyes up, looking straight through the living dead hoards coming straight towards us. I muttered something witty and threw the electric "bomb" into the water, awaiting the sights and sounds of the soon to be frying zombies. A split second before the animatronics kid hit the water, the power went out! The hoard continued coming after us, never knowing what almost happened to them. My movie moment was over. We ran..........fast.

We made our way to a building labeled "Employee's Only". This place looks like a break room for the employees. We have decided to rest here for a while. I don't think any zombie saw us enter here, so we should be safe, at least for now.

Day 65

Just as we were getting comfortable in the employees lounge last night, we heard a crash in one of the back rooms. We decided to go investigate as a group. After wandering around the building for about 20 minutes, we came across a room with a locked door. We could hear noises coming from behind the door. I wanted to just leave; bad things happen to people that investigate strange noises. Dustin, Tonya, and Cole all wanted to see what it was. Their curiosity getting the best of them, they voted and decided to open the door with or without my consent. After looking around a little more, we found a crowbar lying beside an old tool box. I grabbed a large pipe wrench and prepared for the worst.

Dustin put the crowbar into the door jam and counted...1.....2......3. The door flew open, ripping away from the hinges by the power of the crowbar. Inside the room were hundreds or thousands of costumes. We slowly entered the room, carefully walking down the cramped isle towards the back. We walked just a few feet into the room, when a zombie lunged out from between two costumes. The zombie looked to be in her mid to late 20's. She had long blond hair that was caked in dirt and blood. Her eyes were the normal zombie white and her skin color was a light blue-grey. She was wearing one of the cartoon characters outfits, minus the hat that would cover her head. The sight was both frightening as well as a little humorous. The speed at which she moved was not funny at all. I have never seen a zombie move as fast as she did. I really hope that is not a sign of things to come.

She moved fast, but she didn't get very far before Dustin's Titanium crowbar came crashing down across the side of her face. The blow was enough to knock her down, but she was still "alive". I drove the wrench down onto her head. With my blow, her skull had split open like a melon. After searching the room, we found a letter, presumably, written by the girl. We took the letter and closed the door behind us.

We decided to stay in that building one more night. Tomorrow I will post the letter she wrote. Tonight we are going to rest as much as we can; zombies moving as fast as she did scare the hell out of me. I need to try to clear my head and prepare for what we may face in the near future.

Day 66

The girls note, written on the back of an OSHA poster,

"I am going to die soon. I know this, because I have been bitten by one of those things. I have decided to lock myself in this room, so I cannot hurt anyone. For a long time it has only been myself and my boyfriend. We have been surviving on anything we could find. Since the outbreak began, we have been in this damn theme park, hoping someone would come rescue us. Day after day, week after week, we had been waiting for someone....anyone to come help us. Two weeks ago, my boyfriend Shaughn went for help; he never came back.
I went looking for food a few days ago and came across a group of those things. I fought them off as much as I could, but one of them bit me on my leg. I got away, but I know what happens when you get bit. I saw my family change right before my eyes. Now I guess I am going to be joining them. I don't know how long I have left. Shaughn, if you find this letter, please know that I love you and I am sorry for anything I may have done in the past.

Ok, it has been two days since I got bit. I feel really bad. My mouth is so dry and my stomach feels like it is being ripped apart from the inside. My head has never hurt so badly either. I am so cold. I am going to put on this stupid animal suit hopefully it will help warm me up a little.

I don't know how much more I am going to be able to write. My hands are cramping up so bad. I have been vomiting all night and all day, even though nothing comes up except for some blood every now and then. I never thought it would end like this. I was going to be a lawyer. I miss Shaughn.

So cold...so sick...won't last much longer...things are getting dark...
I hear people in the other room...I must be hallucinating now...I think I'm going to sleep for a little bit now..."

She must have changed right after we arrived. Poor girl....we will never know her name.

Day 67

We were awoken early this morning by the sounds of explosions in the city. The explosions rocked the walls and knocked things over throughout the room we were in. It felt like a big earthquake that just would not end. I ran over to the door to see if I could see anything going on outside. When I looked outside, large pillars of black smoke were rising from the heart of the city. From behind the building, flew five jets. They flew directly towards the city. Once they were right at the edge of the city, they all let their rockets fly. Three large buildings were destroyed within seconds! Within another few seconds, five more jets roared above us, heading in the same direction. Tonya let out a yelp of happiness. She yanked Cole up and began hugging him. Dustin patted me on the back. "It's just about over buddy!" he kept saying to me. A great relief swept over me; it will all be over soon. This is the first I had seen the military since all this began. The military to the rescue! I don't know why, but I feel like everything is going to be OK now. Those zombies are fucked now! The US military, the best the world has ever known, is about to open up all hell on them.

We sat back and watched them destroy the city I had once loved. All day long they have been bombing the city. It's the biggest fireworks display I have ever seen. Every two of three minutes five more jets come in to drop their payload on the city. Tonya made a large sign on the roof, so one of the jets will know there are survivors on the ground. I am sure they will be heading this way to come get us. From up on the roof, we have been laughing at the zombies we feared the past couple months. These poor bastards have no idea of what is going to happen to them. My bet is that in a day or two, the ground troops will sweep through here, blasting any remaining undead creature they see. They will rescue us, taking us to their secure base. Yeah, everything is going to be just fine. Hahaha! I bet Darcy is sitting at the base now, waiting for me to arrive. Yeah, I know she isn't expecting me, but I know she will be so surprised seeing me step off the military helicopter. We have made it! We have survived! Things are definitely going to get better.

Day 68

The explosions are still going on. No one slept much last night due to the "light show". Every few minutes another wave of attacks would come bursting overhead. It looks like the planes are getting closer to us though. I am sure they have seen us by now though. Today a helicopter flew really close to us, I could see them looking down at us. We have been celebrating most of the afternoon. Every time a bomb goes off, we cheer. Some zombies have made their way to our location. I'm not sure how many there are, but we're not worried. The ground troops will surely come get us very soon. Ah! Even as I am writing this, I see three helicopters making their way towards us. This could be it! This could be the day we are rescued!!

The helicopters are circling our position. They have waved at us!!!! We are saved!

OH CHRIST! They are shooting at us! Dustin has been grazed with a bullet. Why??!? Why would they do this to us? We are survivors. I have to get somewhere safer than this place. The bullets are coming through the ceiling.

Day 69

Things have gone from bad to worse. Dustin is hurt pretty bad. The bullet ripped through his right arm. We bandaged him up with some old rags we found laying around in the costume room. He is hurt, but I think he will be fine. None of us know what is going on. The military is supposed to be on our side! They are supposed to be here helping us!

We made our way out of the building last night, moving quickly over the ripped apart bodies of the zombies. As we stepped over the bodies, some were still moving, trying in vain to bite us as we passed. It was hard to see, but I remember kicking a severed head across the street like a soccer ball; it bounced across the road, coming to a rest with a squish and a thud. Cole began laughing and slipped on a pile of intestines. As he was getting up, the body attached to the intestines began making its way towards him. All that was left from the body was the upper torso and a few organs. Cole jumped up, kicked the half zombie in the teeth and jumped over him. We all ran as fast as we could though the rest of the way through the theme park. As we got to the far end, we helped each other over the fence and down into a sewage drain. We followed the drain as far as we could, until we came to an opening directly in front of a large subdivision. Just as we emerged from the drain tube, two jets unloaded their ammo on the theme park, within seconds, reducing it to a pile of burning rubble, ash, and twisted metal.

We ran towards the nearest house, to catch our breath. As we turned the corner, to move towards the front of the house, we could now see the city in all its burning glory. The site of the city is more than I can describe. I remember seeing a movie when I was a kid about what a town looks like after a nuclear war; this was worse.....much worse. The sorties the military flew on their bombing runs had taken its toll on the city. At one time, there were so many skyscrapers you could not see the sky. Now, where we are, just over a mile away from downtown, we can see no skyscrapers. The whole area is covered by smoke and fire.

We all sat in a flower garden with our backs against the front wall of one of the houses. No one said anything. We all just sat and watched the city burn. I felt sick. The zombies want to eat us, the military wants to kill us, and the city is a desolate wasteland. Just when I was beginning to think things couldn't get any worse, it began to rain.

Day 70

The rain continued on throughout the night and into most of today. Thankfully, the air strikes have stopped. We found some shelter in one of the houses in the neighborhood. The house is a nice brick five bedroom home crammed right in between two other houses. The houses look just the same; like so many other neighborhoods located on the outskirts of the city. From the pictures hung around the house, this was a family of four. The perfect little family, mom, dad, and the son and daughter; they were probably lawyers or something similar. All the house was missing was the little picket fence to make it the true "American Dream" home.

After we checked out the house, I called a meeting; we needed to figure out what we were going to do. There was little debate about whether or not we should go ahead and make our way through the city. We have to get as far away from the city as possible and the only way to get away from the city is to go back the way we came, or go around it which could take several days. After much debate we decided to go straight through and take our chances on the burning city as opposed to fighting our way around. The way I figure it, most of the zombies will be blow to pieces because of the blasts, so it should be the safest route. I am also hoping the military will decide to bomb somewhere else since they have already destroyed the city. We gathered some supplies from the house and are planning on heading out first thing in the morning. I am hoping we can get deep into the city tomorrow. All we have to do is make it to the other side of the city and then about 15 miles and I am home. I hope I have a home. There is an Air Force base less than two miles away from my home. At this point, I am not even sure why I am going home; it has been 70 days. Darcy would have run out of food by now, if she survived the initial wave of the undead. I have little hope of her being alive. I guess it is this gut feeling I have that she is OK. Hope for her being alive is the only thing I have to live for….it is what I have been fighting for.

Tonya just came into the room to tell us that she saw someone walking on the side of the house. I now see him also. He is looking in the windows of the house right beside us. He just turned and is looking directly at me. Friend or foe, I guess we will soon find out.

Day 71

When the stranger looked at us in the window, he saw me looking directly at him, so he ran. Dustin, Cole, and I all ran after him; if he was military, he would tell the others where we were. Cole, being the skinny kid that he is, got to him first. He kicked the strangers' feet out from under him, causing him to flip head over heels, before coming to a stop. We surrounded the guy, ready to pounce if necessary. I could tell he was scared; I could also tell he was certainly not military. He had dyed black hair and black fingernail polish on, though most of it had been scratched off. He kept begging us not to kill him. Once we got him calmed down, he shocked us all by introducing himself as Shaughn. He said he had to get back to his girlfriend that was waiting for him at the amusement park! We didn't know what to say; how do you tell someone their girlfriend was turned into a zombie, so we killed her? We said nothing about her.

    Shaughn told us what it was like in the city before the military strike as well as the conditions on the other side of the city. He told us about the hundreds or thousands of zombies that were covering the streets in the city. He said he made it through the city (just barely) and made his way to the Air Force base, where armed guards were posted inside the fence, with instructions to kill anything that approached. He told how he watched soldiers open fire on an unarmed family that was trying to get to safety on the base. He said after seeing that, he knew it was time to head back and to stay far away from the base. He decided to go around the city instead of taking a chance on going through it again. Had he gone through the city, he would have been nothing more than burning flesh right now. After talking with us for a few hours, he said he needed to get back to his girlfriend, to see if she had survived the bombings. We let him go without telling him of her fate. No one said anything until he was long gone. Tonya stared at a picture of a stormy ocean and water crashing on the sharp rocks that was hung on the wall behind the couch. After a few minutes, she looked directly at me and said "we should have told him", and then she left the room. In another life and in another time I would have told him. For today though, I will let him discover the fate of his girlfriend for himself.

Day 72

We decided to go ahead with our plan and make our way through the city and head towards my house. We all agreed that we would avoid the military base at all costs. Traveling has been slow today because of the destroyed terrain. The city looks so alien now, with all the buildings destroyed and on fire. We only made it a few miles before we had to stop for a break. We found an old convenience store that looked to be mostly intact and decided to stay here for the rest of the day. The only zombies we have seen today have been severely wounded to the point of only being able to crawl around. The ones we came across, we would destroy and put out of their misery. The whole place was covered in soot and ash for as far as the eye could see, which because of the ever increasing smoke, wasn't very far.

From the room I am in, I can see what used to be a

bus station. All the windows have been blown out and the roof has caved in. You can see three or four dead people/zombies lying under the rubble, their hands burnt and broken. The smell of the burning city is enough to make even the strongest stomachs turn inside out. I don't know if it is the smell of all the burning flesh or the smell of all the rotting corpses; hell, it is probably a combination of both. In order to block the stench, we have tied rags around our faces so we all look like bank robbers from the Old West times. Great, now we're playing cowboys and zombies!
In the back ground, we can hear helicopters flying around. I am thinking our best bet is going to be to find somewhere underground; maybe a sewage system, anything to get us off the roads (or what is left of them); if there even is a sewage system anymore. If you listen closely, you can just barely hear the faint unmistakable moans of the living dead. Though the sounds are faint, they seem to be getting stronger as the day goes on.

Machinegun fire can now be heard off in the distance. From the sounds, it seems to be coming from the helicopters. Part of me is happy for them taking out as many zombies as they can, but the other part hates them, knowing that they may be taking out survivors as well. The helicopter does not sound right. It sounds like it is having some mechanical troubles.

Oh! The helicopter crashed. There was a loud explosion that shook the building we are in. Dustin and the others want to go check it out, so it looks like we are going to head that way. If nothing else, maybe we can find some weapons.

Day 73

We didn't have any trouble finding the downed helicopter; all we had to do was follow the ball of flames. When we arrived at the crash site, it was hard to determine what was helicopter and what was building. The copter crashed into a destroyed office building, breaking apart all the way to the ground. As we got closer, we could see the pilot hunched over the controls, his head almost completely removed just above the mouth. The co pilot was impaled by a metal rod from the building. We quickly removed a few weapons we found laying beside the copter then began to head back to the convenience store, when we heard a cry for help. We had no intention of helping, these people had tried to kill us just a day or two earlier, but Tonya, being the caring person that she is, could not just let them die, no matter what they may have tried to do.

The first person we came to was a soldier laying about 50 feet away from the downed craft. He was laying face down in on the ground; both arms looked to be broken. He was very bloodied, but alive. Dustin and I carefully turned him over onto his back. His nose was broken and he was missing his front teeth. As we began checking him for any additional injuries, I felt a hard piece of metal jam into the back of my neck. From behind me I heard a man's voice telling me to "get the hell away from him". I turned to see a soldier wearing full chem. gear, gas mask and all, holding am M -16 to my throat. I tried explaining to him that we were just trying to help. Either he was not listening to me or he did not care; either way, he was not budging. I threw my hand in the air and backed away from the hurt soldier. Less than two seconds after I backed away, a white hand and flashed out from under a downed wall. The hand grabbed the downed soldier and yanked him half way under the wall. The soldier began to scream in agony and pain. Dustin grabbed the soldier by the shirt, pulling on him as hard as he could to get him away from the feasting zombie. He pulled one last time with all his might and the soldier came sliding back out, only this time, it was only the top half of his body. The soldier behind me yelled in anger, pulled a grenade from his belt and lobbed it toward the wall. As the grenade hit the ground, we all ran; everyone except Dustin. He just stood by the wall, holding the now dead half soldier in his hands. The grenade exploded less than two feet away from Dustin. The grenade scrap metal ripped through Dustin's body and destroyed half the downed wall. With the sounds of the explosion still ringing in my ears, I looked around to see Tonya crying and running towards Dustin's lifeless body. Cole was lying on the ground beside me; his eyes were wide with the shock of what had just happened. The soldier looked down at Cole and me as he stepped over us, heading towards the wall. When he got to the wall, he pointed the M -16 down and began shooting where the zombie once was. He glanced back at Tonya and Dustin, and then turned towards a pile of rubble on the other side of the downed helicopter. As the sound began returning to my ears, I could hear the horrific sounds of the undead approaching. I scrambled to my feet, helped Cole up, and then went to help Tonya. She was holding Dustin's limp body in her arms and rocking back and forth "I am sick of all this death", she said over and over again. I tried to calm her down as best I could. I assured her I would do my best to shield her from any more death. I lied. I had to; we had to get out of there and in a hurry. We all three made our way quickly back to the store. As I was closing the door behind us, I scanned around to make sure no zombie eyes had seen us make our escape.

Looks like another night of silence. Silence other than the occasional scream and quick burst of machine gun fire in the distance.

Day 74

The screams and machine gun fire tapered off late last night, until it was nothing more than machine gun fire; then nothing. We are not sure which was worse, the noise or the lack of. We had every intention on heading out today, but we changed our minds when we saw the number of zombies that passed by our little makeshift shelter. We lost count after about 2000. It looked like an army; an undead army, marching into battle. At first we thought they were wandering around with no place to go, without a direction, until it dawned on us that they were all going in the same direction then entire time. I wonder what they could have been going after.

All day they have been walking by us, totally unaware of our presence. Just about an hour ago, they stopped walking by. Every now and then we will see a straggler or two, but the mass migration has passed for now. We have decided to leave in the morning as long as everything is clear tomorrow.

Day 75

We have guests.

The migration had ended, so we packed up everything and started to leave. As we were about to walk out the door/hole in the wall, in walked two soldiers carrying a third injured one. We scared them as much as they scared us, the only difference is they had machine guns already in the ready position. That now makes two times in the past three days that I have had a gun pointed at my head!

    The soldiers began screaming at us to lay on the grounds with our arms and legs spread out wide. We had no choice but to comply. This new breed of military is "shoot first, ask questions later, if ever". They were all wearing gas masks and suits that resembled shark dive suits. The one who appeared to be in charge walked up to us and asked if any one of us had been bitten or scratched by one of them. The soldier asked if anyone was sick or feeling ill at all. Once we said no, the soldier ordered us to stand up and remove all our clothes. We just stood there for a moment. We were not about to just strip down naked in front of anyone! The soldiers prepping and turning the safety off their guns made us change our minds rather quickly. The leader of the group laughed a little and said "trust me boys, you have nothing to worry about, you're not my type." As the words passed over the lips of the leader, the soldier removed the gas mask to reveal a woman with blond almost white hair pulled back into a pony tail. She walked in front of all of us, looking very closely at our bodies; inspecting for any bite marks. As she passed by each of us, she would make snide remarks, giggle a little, and then tell us to get dressed. When she got in front of Tonya, she said to her "Now you are definitely my type". Without warning, Tonya slapped the leader very hard across her face. The slap forced her to take a couple steps back. The other solders pointed their guns directly at Tonya with every intention to blow her head off. The leader began to laugh and told

Tonya to get dressed. The soldiers lowered their weapons. Once we were all dressed, the leader introduced herself and her soldiers. She said her name was Alisha and she was a reservist that got a call to report for duty at the base right before the zombies started appearing. The other soldier, the uninjured one, introduced himself as Jeremiah. He said he had been stationed at the base in South America where everything first started. He told a long story about the first few days of the uprising, that I will relay later. Alisha introduced the injured soldier as Ed. He was also a reservist that got the call to report at the same time as Alisha. Ed was injured, but not severely. His foot had been crushed when the helicopter crashed and his ribs are bruised but he was able to walk on his own with a slight limp. Alisha said she recognized us from the crash site and said she was sorry for our loss. She didn't have to say who she was talking about; we knew she was meant Dustin.

    We have spent the majority of the day talking about the state the world is in. It does not look good for humanity. We are losing the battle.

    Tonya doesn't trust the soldiers at all. She wants us to leave them as fast as possible, but I think they may be able to help me get closer to home.
Only time will tell.

Day 76

Last night, Jeremiah told us his account of the first few days of the virus in South America. I know I am going to forget a few details, but this is how I remember it as he relayed it to me.

Jeremiah told us he had been stationed in South America for the past few years. He said he was the first one to arrive at the scene when they found that little kid (Shawn Crockett). His picture was splashed all over the magazines such as Time and US Weekly. The picture was him carrying Shawn in his arms into the military hospital. Jeremiah stood guard over the little boy until he died. He was sad to see the little kid pass away, but in his line of work, he had seen quite a few people taken before their time. He said he stood next to the doctors when they held the press conference. He was the first to respond to the "scream that shocked a nation" as it was later called. He told how he ran into the hospital, to see the doctor performing the autopsy laying dead in a pool of blood; his throat ripped out. He said he saw Shawn licking the blood off the ground; his eyes now a cold white color, his skin pale to match. When Shawn saw Jeremiah standing in the door, he immediately began walking towards him. By that time, the room was full of doctors and other military personnel.

Two people were checking on the autopsy doctor when the doctor suddenly "woke up". The doctor bit into the arms of both the people assisting. Jeremiah turned and began shooting the autopsy doctor, to no avail. The doctor continued to bite people in the room, taking a chunk out of anyone standing in his path. Finally, a stray bullet ripped through the doctors' head, killing him instantly, for good. During all the commotion, Shawn managed to slip out the door and he in turn also began biting unsuspecting bystanders. By the time Shawn was "taken out" completely, a total of 37 people had been bitten. Jeremiah said they tried to contain the situation, but with that many people, a few who had been bitten had managed to escape the quarantine of the hospital.

Soon after, the whole city had to be quarantined, and then the state, and shortly thereafter, the whole country. No commercial airlines were allowed in or out of South America, only military flights. Large gates were erected along the border and guards were posted every few feet to ensure no one left the quarantine area. Hundreds of people were shot as they attempted to cross the barricades. Thousands of the undead were also shot as they made their way towards the fences.

Jeremiah was one of the last ones out of the country. (First in, Last out; that was their motto). When he finally left the country, he said they had left under duress, because the base had been overrun with the infected. When he arrived in the U.S., he was greeted with the same strip down procedure that we were given.

It appeared that the US government had contained the virus to just South America, until mass murders and a large amount of "rabies" cases began springing up all over the country. That was when the government realized the virus was unstoppable. The virus spread so fast in the states that the military was forced to abandon all posts and convene in to two or three strongholds. One of those bases just happened to be the one down the road from my house!

Jeremiah told us their orders were to shoot and kill anything or anyone that approached the base. They maintained those orders, until they realized they were going to lose the base unless they began fighting back. He said the other bases had stopped transmitting a few weeks ago, so it is assumed our base is the only one left. That is when the base commander decided to go on a seek and destroy mission. Anything that moved was a target. People could not be trusted anymore, so anyone not on the base was to be shot on sight; no exceptions. He was on the helicopter that began firing on us while we were on the building at the amusement park. He said he had asked to rescue us, but was given an order to fire and take us out. He said he missed us on purpose, but was instructed to fly back out to the city and take out anything left alive (or undead). As they returned to the city, their copter began having technical problems and went down. He said they fought off dozens of zombies that managed to survive the massive attack, but eventually got over run, so they fled, looking for any kind of shelter.

Finally, Jeremiah told us about the military strikes around the base. He said they bombed every square inch of land in a 25 square mile radius of the base. My house is within that radius! I asked him about that area. He shook his head and whispered "all gone, it's all been leveled".

I am crushed.

Any chance Darcy may have had, is now gone.
I am completely crushed.

Day 77

Ed is beginning to feel a little better now; his wounded foot and ribs are healing very quickly. I spent a good bit of time talking to him today. He told me a little about his family. He said they flew to the base with him and they are safe in one of the bunkers/fallout shelters that are located on the base. Ed told me how they allowed some locals on the base right before everything "went to shit". That gave me a glimmer of hope. I had thought once before about the shelters, now this just confirms what I had hoped. Maybe Darcy got lucky and was in one of the bunkers, safely locked underground with plenty of food and water that can last years.

Alisha walked around the perimeter of the building

most of the night and attempted to contact the military base. All that came across the airwaves was static. At this point, we don't know if the radios are busted or if the base as been over run or if the base has cut off all contact now that the squad has been "contaminated". We don't know if we now have to watch our backs of if we should look to the military for help. I am not sure which is going to be worse, if the military is after us now, or if there is no military left at all. If a mass migration hit the base, there are not enough fences and bullets to stop them all. There were around four million people living in the city at the time of the uprising. If even half of those are now zombies, that is a lot of people attacking one little fortified base.

Cole and Tonya sat in a corner talking about our options with Jeremiah most of the morning. I can see the mistrust written all over Tonya's face. Every suggestion Jeremiah comes up with, Tonya finds some reason why the plan wouldn't work. I see her getting very frustrated at times, because she knows a plan is good, but does not want to admit it. I just hope she can drop her attitude by the time a real decision needs to be made.

I have been sitting back watching everyone. I can't help but laugh a little at our little family.

That is what we have become now, a family; Tonya, Cole, and myself. We watch each other at all times. No one goes anywhere without one of us going with them. We have grown closer to one another over the past few weeks or months. I would do anything for them and I believe they would do anything for me. I know that no matter what happens, we will all watch out for each other. I wish I could relay this to Tonya right now, to let her know that I got her back and I am here for her, and that she has nothing to worry about.

Alisha just came in; it looks like another mass migration is heading our way. She said it is the largest mass of undead she has ever seen.

Tonight should be interesting.

Day 78

To say the migration was large would be a HUGE understatement. There were (and still are) massive amounts of the undead walking past us. All night last night we saw wave after wave of them. They are moving at a slow pace, but every now and then they will show a quick burst of speed.

We have been lying low to the ground, not moving at all, just staying in one spot. We were smart enough to cover ourselves in the blood from a few zombies we killed that were behind the building we are in. I am worried though, because the blood is drying up and starting to flake up and peel off. If the migration doesn't slack off soon, we will be in for one hell of a fight.

The moans are the worst part of all this. They really take their toll on our sanity. I remember the first gulf war and how we (the US army) would play loud rock music over and over at high levels, trying to force the Iraqi people out of their compounds. I really feel like this is somewhat of a strategy of the undead. If it is, it is working. Cole is lying next to me. I can hear him as he groans every few minutes. He has his hands over his ears. I have been attempting to convince him to try to ignore it; reminding him of the other times we have had to survive and live with the moans happening all around us.

It is hard to convince someone it is going to be ok and that it will be over soon, when I, myself, don't believe it. I am not sure how the moans are affecting anyone else, because we are all spread out. Cole is directly beside me, while Tonya and the others are scattered around the room. Shit, Ed just coughed! It looks like a couple zombies heard it and they are headed this way!

Day 79

It was a close call; too close of a call.

As the zombies began making their way towards the shelter we were hiding in, a scream could be heard from across the street. A woman was standing on the side of the road screaming at the undead migration as it passed. Three people came running out after her, trying to drag her back inside their shelter. Within seconds, the three of them were completely surrounded by thousands of zombies. Another couple seconds later and they were nothing more than shreds of flesh, bone, and blood. It looked like they were put into a wood chipper. Once the majority of the bodies were devoured, a few of the zombies were licking the blood off the road like a dog. The whole process took less than three minutes! The only good that came from the slaughter was that we were spared from that same fate; every zombie in the city was trying to get a piece of them, ignoring a maybe for a sure thing.

The rest of the day and evening and even into this morning the migration continued. It finished just a few hours ago, ending the parade of the dead with a few corpses dragging their mutilated bodies along the ground with their hands. We waited for maybe an hour for any additional stragglers to come a long before we came out of hiding. We all emerged feeling like the luckiest people in the world. Jeremiah walked over and punched Ed in the shoulder as hard as he could for the sneeze. We stood around in complete shock as to what we had just witnessed the past few days. We could not believe the ferocity and the speed at which the zombies mutilated the three people.

As we were standing around talking, we saw someone walking out of the building the other three people had come out of. It was Shaughn. He walked out of the building, walked up to the blood stain on the ground and looked around at his surroundings. While he was looking around, he didn't notice a zombie coming up behind him from around the corner of the building. Jeremiah and I both jumped up and ran towards the opening of our shelter. Alisha, who was standing by the opening, ran out the door ahead of us, screaming for Shaughn to get out of the way. As he turned around, he was knocked over by the creature hungry for his blood. Shaughn grabbed the zombie by the throat and lower jaw, keeping its mouth as far away from any part of his body as possible. As Shaughn raised the zombies head up in the air, Alisha came from across the street, striking the zombie across the nose with the butt of her rifle. The zombies' neck snapped back, breaking every bone holding his head up. His body rolled backwards a few times before coming to a complete stop against the building. The zombie was lying with his stomach against the building, upside down, with his head looking directly back at us. The sight was very unnatural and a little strange. Without saying a word to Shaughn, Alisha walked directly up to the zombie, who was now attempting to stand up, and stepped on his neck, pinning his head to the ground. With the rifle still in her hand, she began beating the zombie in the face repeatedly, until all that was left was a pool of red Jell-O. We all sat back in amazement at her brutality, more impressed than horrified.

Shaughn was too exhausted to tell us what had happened since we had last seen him, so we didn't push the subject. We let him sleep, which is where he is now, I am anxious to hear his story tomorrow.

Day 80

Our excitement for Shaughn's story quickly faded into nothing more than a distant memory this morning by a sudden unexpected attack.

Jeremiah was on guard, while the rest of us slept. I had just fallen asleep when I was jolted awake by the sounds of a loud crash. Everything happened to fast. Since it was so dark, it was nearly impossible to see anything going on. A small sliver of moonlight crept through one of the cracks in the wall. The light was just enough for me to see Alisha, Cole, and Ed run out the back. Jeremiah was lying on his back, with two zombies on top of him. Shaughn was standing behind one of the zombies with a knife slicing deep into the ghouls' neck. I jumped to my feet as quickly as I could, only to be knock back down by a zombie two times my size. I could see three more zombies desperately trying to get into the shelter. I had no time to think, only to react. I rolled over onto my side and kicked the shit out of the approaching zombie; he didn't budge. I scrambled to my feet in just enough time to dodge an oncoming attack from an infected mouth. I had no idea what to do! I was way over powered and the speed at which he was moving took me aback. He had me pinned in a corner, with nowhere to run. As he began to pounce, a loud shotgun blast removed the zombies left side of his face. Two more shots and all the zombies in the room were lying dead on the ground. Everything in the room stopped for a brief second, long enough for me to run out the back, along with Jeremiah, Shaughn and this new person wearing a ski mask a deadly accurate shotgun aim.

    As we ran out the back, we were followed by a group of about 20 more zombies. We caught a quick glimpse of Alisha and the others, so we went to their location. Once we arrived, our rest was very short lived, because of the pursuing group of undead heading our way. The shotgun person waved the gun in the air and yelled for us to follow. Because we had nowhere else to go, we had no choice. The shotgun person led us to the entrance of the old maximum security prison facility. Once there, the large metal gates slid open slowly and just enough to allow us entry. Once inside, the gate quickly slid closed, trapping us in some sort if "holding" area. The person with the shotgun turned to face us and removed the mask to reveal it was a woman. She wore a Prison guard uniform with a broken name tag. The name tag read "Mego", the rest had been broken off. She had one shotgun in her hand and another one strapped to her back. Around her waist she wore a gun belt with three pistols strapped to it. She stood in front of us, sweating and breathing heavy from the run. She whistled to someone inside, who opened the next set of door to allow us access. As we stepped inside, we were shocked to see a group of about 20 people. They looked thin and scared, but happy to be alive. "Mego" told us to all take a break and relax for a while. She showed us to a couple cells that she said we could use for shelter for as long as we liked. Once we were alone, everyone picked out a section of the cell and collapsed from exhaustion. I could not sleep, so I decided to write about what had happened today.

I just heard "Mego" tell someone that they were going to have a "prison meeting" in the morning. I am not sure what that means and frankly, I am too tired to care. I will wait till tomorrow to be concerned. As of right now, I am just going to enjoy the slight safety.

Day 81

The compound.

We all woke up at around the same time this morning. Having gotten a good amount of sleep, we were very anxious to see our surroundings. We felt like strangers in a strange land. We wandered through the halls of the old prison, until we found "Mego". She was sitting in the Wardens office, watching security cameras, drinking Captain Morgan's Rum straight out of the bottle and eating Gummy bears. She welcomed us in to the office and asked us to sit down. Once we were seated, she began telling us a little about herself. She was a prison guard at that very facility when everything started. She said they locked the place down, hoping to avoid any infection in the prison, but like everything else needing to stay out of a prison, somehow the infection got in. She said her and other fellow guards attempted to contain those infected by locking them in cells below the prison, but eventually it got out of hand. She said she is the only survivor left. The others had abandoned their posts or were infected themselves. After clearing the main prison from the living dead, she decided to turn it into a sanctuary for any survivors she could find. She said there are still zombie inmates in the bottom part of the prison, but they are well secured. "Mego" told us that during the air strike one part of the prison had been destroyed, but they blocked that part off and have two people guarding the spot at all times. She said they have no food reserves, so they have to go out scavenging for food whenever they can. She showed us on one of her monitors a little patch of ground that used to be a recreation area that is now used for growing plants. She said their plan is to stay in that shelter and let the zombies outside starve to death.

I like her plan, but I fear that we are just rats in a cage in here. If the zombies found out about the amount of people living in here, they would be all over this place, forcing their way in here and we would have no place to run. I have already begun plotting our escape, not that we are prisoners, but I just have a really bad feeling about this place. The whole place kind of creeps me out.

"Mego" told us there are 37 people staying here. She said they are survivors from around the city that she found a few at a time while she was out looking for food. We just happened to be the latest ones found. As I was glancing around the room, I saw people in the guard towers, with rifles and people walking up and down the prison inner walls. It was as if we were in a military base, or a well guarded compound in another country. "Mego" flipped a switch on one of the monitors to reveal a room full of zombies. There must have been 200 or more. They were all in a large dark room. I heard Tonya gasp a little at the site. I felt very uncomfortable and judging by the looks on Ed and Jeremiahs face, I could tell they were none too happy either. "Mego" assured us they are completely locked away with no chance of escaping.

During all of this, Cole stared out the window. He didn't say anything, just continued to stare. I got up to check on him. When I got to the window, I saw what had drawn his attention. From where we were in the prison, we could see over the entire city(what was left of it anyway) and beyond. Just past our location, heading straight towards the military base, was a very large mass of undead people. They looked like ants in the distance....ants or more like a cloud, a dark black cloud. There were millions of them, as far in either direction as you can see. Cole looked up at me and asked "what are we going to do?" I had no answer for him or no good answer, all I could do was grab him by the arm and whisper "survive".

Day 82

We stood by the window yesterday for hours, staring at the "black cloud", wondering how we were going to make it; how we were going to survive in a world completely over run with zombies. Where can we go when everything around us is destroyed and when everyone is trying to get us? As we watched the millions of zombies, there was a huge explosion seen in the distance. Ed took a step back. He shook his head and said "That's the base....we have nowhere to go now." "Mego" started laughing and pulled us away from the window. She walked back to the desk, plopped her feet up on the desk and continued eating as if nothing had happened. We quickly excused ourselves and went on to tour the rest of the facility.

The rest of the day was rather boring; we walked around and met a few people staying in the compound. There were people from every walk of life, from the very poor to the very rich (or at one time they were rich). We met a doctor named Kenneth, who lost everything, including his whole family during the first wave of the undead. He said "Mego" found him wandering around the streets of the city over a month ago. He was a very angry and "glass half empty" kind of guy. For some reason, being around him reminded me of being around Roger. We met a really nice family from West Virginia, who just happened to be visiting the city when everything happened. They had stayed together as a family and together they have survived. They were very thankful for everything they have and were very optimistic about the future. Cole met some girls that he seemed to have an instant crush on; they were just about his age, but after everything that had happened, a few years difference wouldn't really matter. I didn't have the heart to tell him not to get too comfortable, since we would be leaving in a few days. With a group of zombies as large as we had seen in the distance, being in this area was the worst place we could be.

I went to bed early last night and awoke early this morning. I have been enjoying the nice quiet life so far today. Alisha and Tonya have been getting to know each other today and I get the feeling they are quickly becoming friends. Ed and Jeremiah have decided to go down to the basement/ lower lock up levels, to ensure there are no escapes from the zombie inmates. Hopefully things can settle down a bit before we have to leave.

Day 83

I am beginning to get the feeling "Mego" does not want us to leave. I mentioned it to her late last night. She didn't say we couldn't go, but she tried everything she could to talk me in to staying. She said we (the human race) needs to stay together, to repopulate the world once the zombies are gone. Now, I for one completely agree. We do need to stick together, but far away from the city area. I give it a few more days before the zombies find out our location and decide they want in here. We need to get some place safe. I don't know whether that means the desert, the arctic, or some tropical island, but I know we can't stay here. These walls may keep a couple hundred or even a couple thousand out, but it would never hold up against the millions out there. I don't know if it is safe anywhere.

I thanked "Mego" for her hospitality, but told her we (meaning myself and anyone who wanted to go with me) would be leaving soon. She just laughed and put her arm around me and said "I'm sure you'll change your mind soon honey."

    I slept in a little this morning, since I was up so late last night. When I awoke this morning, I was greeted by Kenneth and Tonya. They were standing on the other side of door to my "room" whispering and arguing as quietly as they could. As I walked around the corner, they immediately stopped talking and were silent, clearly startled by my presence. Tonya stared down at the ground, while Kenneth stared at me as if he had something to say. When I asked them what was going on, Kenneth began to say something, but stopped short by Tonya's sharp glance. He mumbled "nothing" and began walking away. As he was reaching the end of the hall to head out of sight, he turned his head around and yelled at Tonya "Then you tell him." My gaze instantly went to Tonya, who looked as if she were about to explode with anger.

    It took a good 10 minutes before Tonya began telling me what was going on. As I write this, I am filled with every type of emotion imaginable. Hopeful is the best way to describe it. I am hopeful in the face of insurmountable odds, but hopeful none the less. I need to go find Kenneth now, so I can find out exactly what he knows, but as of now, I do know that he saw Darcy in the city the very day "Mego" found him! He said she was carrying around my picture and was showing it to everyone. Tonya said Kenneth instantly recognized me, but wanted to wait until the time was right to tell me.

That is all Tonya would tell me.

Kenneth has to fill in the blanks about this right NOW.

Day 84

Kenneth's story

I tracked down Kenneth yesterday and pretty much penned him to a chair, forcefully "asking" him to tell me what he knew about Darcy. I tried to be calm about it, but when you have all but given up hope for finding someone then out of nowhere you find out someone knows something about it, there is no stopping you from getting that information. Luckily for Kenneth, he was very willing to talk about what had happened. I was a little surprised by what he had to say.

Shortly after the uprising began, he and a few coworkers had locked themselves in his office. Things were going fine until they ran out of food. Kenneth sent his nurse out to find food; she never returned. Next he sent one of his interns, who also never returned. Finally he decided to go himself. While out looking for food, the doctor encountered quite a few zombies, who, as he put it, met their match and were destroyed.

(Now let me just say that the way he described the fights between himself and the zombies sounded really good, but they also seemed a little extravagant, so take the fighting stories with a grain of salt.)

SO Kenneth continued to tell about his fighting with the zombies...

He walked into a grocery store, it was silent, so he made his way down the canned food isle, when he was completely surrounded by the undead. He ran towards the first group, slid on the ground, tripping the two zombies in his path. Once they were down, he jumped to his feet, grabbed a broom that was propped up against one of the shelves and impaled both zombies through the chest. Next he went after the three remaining zombies. He said he grabbed an arm full of cans and began throwing them at the zombies, knocking them down one by one. Once down, he crushed their skulls in with his foot (!) Next he grabbed a shopping cart and filled it full of food and bottles of water, fighting his way out of the store all along the way.
When he got outside, he said he pushed the cart into the street and heard a noise behind him. When he turned around, he was face to face with the impaled zombies. Thinking quick, he reached down and just happened to find a crowbar lying on the ground, where he again impaled the

zombies, this time directly through their heads, killing them once and for all. Just as he was finishing off the zombies, a MAC truck came roaring down the street, slamming into the shopping cart before coming to a screeching stop about 100 feet away. Out of the front of the cab came a scruffy looking man, with long hair. He introduced himself as Malice!!!

In the truck were a group of survivors he had found right outside of the city. Malice told him that he was heading to Florida to find his woman and invited Kenneth to tag along. Kenneth declined but asked Malice to help him get some food to his office. Together they reloaded the shopping cart full of food and loaded up the back of the truck full of food. Kenneth jumped in the cab and along with the other survivors, made their way back to his office. Once there, the survivors helped move the food and water into the break room. While moving groceries, one of the survivors pulled out a picture and asked if Kenneth if he had seen the person in the photo. (That person was me.) Kenneth told Darcy that he had no idea who I was, but promised to help find me.

After a few days, a group of zombies made their way into the office. In the process, three survivors were killed and four others were infected. In the end, Malice, Darcy, Kenneth, and one other survivor got out of the office unharmed, but they were separated. Kenneth, Darcy, and the other survivor went one way, while Malice ran to his truck, leaving the three behind for good.

After about a week, the military came through, shooting almost anything that moved. He stressed the word *almost*, because Darcy and the other survivor (whose name he could not remember), were picked up by a passing patrol one afternoon. The truck stopped, three men jumped out of the truck, grabbed them both and drove off leaving Kenneth in is hiding spot, unseen. That was the last time he had seen Darcy.

A small spark of hope reignited. Maybe she was o.k. Maybe she was taken to the military base and taken to a fallout shelter, the possibilities are endless. She could be anywhere on the base; the base that is under attack right now.

I will leave tomorrow and head straight for the military base, zombie cloud or not!

Day 85

Something's wrong!

As I was gathering my stuff, I heard a loud siren blearing throughout the entire complex. I saw people running around looking very scared. I met Alisha outside my door. She had no idea what was going on either, so together we ran to find "Mego".

When we found her, she was running through one of the halls, heading towards the basement area. She had a complete look of terror on her face. As she passed us, she yelled at us to go grab any weapons we can find and meet her by the door to the basement.

I am currently in my room and wanted to do a quick update as to what was going on. I have a shotgun and two M-9 pistols with LOTS of ammo. Cole is in here with a couple pistols also. I can see a look of unease in his face. I can only imagine something has happened down in the lower levels; some kind of breach. I just hope the alarm hasn't alerted the zombie cloud to our location. I am sure we can contain anything going on downstairs.

SHIT!

Tonya and Jeremiah just came in. All the zombies have escaped from down below and are making their way up towards us!!! Jeremiah said the family from West Virginia is all dead along with most of the others. He said Kenneth is locked in a room just beyond the basement door. No one has seen "Mego" since earlier. Ed and Alisha are down the hall trying to help some of the other survivors. I have to sign off to help. God help us!

Day 86

Trapped like rats.

We are completely trapped. We are right now located in "Mego's" office. Alisha, Ed, and I are in here with "Mego" and a few others I had never met. Jeremiah, Cole, Tonya, and a few others are in an office across the hall from us. Someone is hurt pretty bad over there. All I can here is screaming; screams of agony. Outside the door are close to 200 zombies. They have completely crammed themselves inside the hallway, desperate to get food. They move so quickly when they are hungry, and these bastards are starving; they have been locked in the lower level for a couple months with no food. Their attack surprised everyone. Apparently, someone went down to make sure everything was secure, when a gate opened automatically. "Mego" thinks someone did it on purpose, though I have no idea why anyone would invite these monsters in here.

Think, think, think.

Damn, I have no idea how we are going to get out of this one. Looking out the window, I can see the cloud of zombies. They almost look like they are getting closer to us. Maybe it's just my paranoia. I am thinking about what the worst case scenario could be and that is it. Maybe we could go out swinging (actually, we would have to go out shooting). We all have plenty of weapons; the problem is we have to shoot them in the head to put them down and no one in this room is good enough to get nothing but head shots. My shotgun has enough force for me to tear through some, but once they are on the ground, they can just bite our ankles, and then we're really screwed. We need something to clear the hall way, just enough for us to make an escape out the gate.

Oh hell, the gate! It is controlled by a switch up in one of the towers. In order to open the gate, someone needs to be in the tower pushing the button. But if someone is pushing the button, they will get left behind. There is very little chance someone can get up to the tower, push the button, then get back down to the gate before the zombies get there.

Hell, I don't need to be thinking about that, I need to be coming up with a plan to get us out of this room, then we can come up with something to get us out the gate!

Think, Think, Think...

It has gotten quiet in the other room.

Actually, it got really quiet, then we heard a BANG! I can only assume someone got bitten then began to change, so Jeremiah (or someone else), took them out. I am going to try to talk to the others to see if they can come up with a plan. These doors aren't going to hold up much longer. I guess on the bright side, there is plenty of alcohol in here, so if the end is coming, at least we can drink ourselves into a stupor, so we won't care about getting eaten. There are a few bottles of Golden Grain, and some other bottles of something that smells quite a bit like moonshine. We could have a great night....

Wait!

Why didn't I think of that before??

I have a plan.

Day 87

Dark horizons on the way.

While we were trapped in the prison office, we called out to the others in the room across from us, to make sure they knew the plan. First we gathered all the bottles of alcohol, ripped up the cloth on the chairs and on the curtains so we could make Molotov cocktails. Once all the mini bombs were made, we slowly opened the door and shot all the zombies that were blocking it. Once we cleared the door-way for a brief second, we lit the bottles and threw them as far down the hall as we could, completely covering any and all zombies in the pathway with flames. We quickly closed the door and waited. The frying bastards never even cried out in pain as they cooked. Once again we opened the door and began shooting as many of the undead as we could.

Within a matter of minutes, the sprinklers were triggered, bringing to an end my wonderful plan. The mini fire bombs got us nowhere, except wet. I had no other plan. We had nowhere to go and nothing else we could do. The smell of the once burning flesh right outside the door was almost too much to bear. Someone in the other room began to cry hysterically.

Right when all hope was lost, we heard a noise that both scared the hell out of us and made us rejoice. It was the sound of a machine gun. By the way it sounded, I think it was an M -60. Along with the loud bang, bang, bang of the gun, came the ricocheting bullets. We dove on to the ground and under "Mego's" desk. Bullets ripped through the room we were in, shredding wood as if it were paper. After what seemed like hours, though I know it was less than five minutes, the firing stopped. We crawled out from under the desk, to see the now Swiss cheese like room. The door was completely destroyed as were the walls surrounding the door frame. Bits and pieces of zombie were scattered throughout the room. When we approached the hole in the wall that used to be a door, we saw Kenneth standing at the end of the hall by the stairs. In his arms he held a machine gun with a glowing red barrel, and now completely out of ammo. I couldn't help but laugh. He had ripped the shirt off his back and tied it around his head.

The way he stood in the hallway reminded me of Rambo, though instead of killing terrorists, he slaughtering about 200 zombies. He stood there, triumphantly huffing and trying to catch his breath. Kenneth had done it! He freed us all from certain death.

All the survivors met back up in the hallway. We wanted to gather all our ammo and some supplies together so we could make our way out of the prison. Kenneth motioned for us to follow him.

I don't remember how it happened; all I remember is seeing the absolute horror on Kenneth's face as three arms came out of one of the offices by the stairs. They grabbed him and drug him, kicking and screaming into the office. We couldn't move. We were frozen by the quickness and shock of it all. One second Kenneth was standing there, proud of himself; the hero, the next second, he was gone.

Finally Jeremiah ran to the end of the hall to kill the bastards that had taken our savior, but he slipped on all the blood now completely covering the floor in the hallway. As soon as his body hit the ground, a zombie came out of nowhere, pouncing on top of him, desperately trying to sink it's teeth into his flesh. Cole ran to his aid, before I could stop him. As he ran towards the fallen solder, he began pulling out a knife, a very large knife that would make Crocodile Dundee proud. Cole too slid on the blood, but he steadied himself enough to slide towards the two. Cole came to a halt directly beside Jeremiah. The zombie turned instantly towards Cole. Quickly and without flinching, Cole drove the blade straight into the top of the fiends head, causing him to instantly slump over.

We all carefully headed down the stairs, glancing quickly into the room where Kenneth could be seen being devoured by two zombies. Alisha, who was the last down the hall stopped long enough to place two rounds directly between the eyes of the zombies. Once in the main hall, we made our way towards the front gate. Along the way, we came across a handful of zombies, which we disposed of quickly. As we reached the front gate, "Mego" yelled at us to go stand by the front. She said she would take care of the gate for us. I tried to protest, but she insisted that she knew the prison better than anyone and that she would know other ways out if her escape route got blocked. I couldn't argue with that. Well, I could have argued, but honestly, I was scared. I couldn't step up and be the hero this time; my body and mind wouldn't let me.

As we stood by the front gates, I could see "Mego" briefly in the windows as she crossed into the other rooms. We could see her as she pressed the button, allowing us to make our escape. As she pressed the button, I saw a flash behind her. There were zombies in the room! We could hear "Mego" yell for us to "get the hell out". No one wanted to leave her, but we had the chance for freedom, so we ran. We ran and never looked back.

We made our way to a parking garage that had been almost completely destroyed on one side. We climbed up the fallen concrete and made our way to the top. From that height, we could see the prison in one direction and the zombie cloud making its way towards us in the other. Behind the zombie cloud was a very dark storm cloud, making its way towards us also.
I have a sinking feeling.

Day 88

It rained all day today and the zombie cloud seemed to get bigger and bigger the closer it got to us. We spent the entire night last night debating on what to do. Most of us think we should stay here and wait out the oncoming zombies. I think we can cover ourselves in zombie blood and keep hidden for a few days; they should pass right by us without ever noticing our presence. A hand full of others want to leave and try to attempt to get out of the area without being seen, before the zombie cloud gets here. I am not going to stop anyone that wants to leave. It is up to them individually. I think it is suicide leaving this area right now. The cloud is probably less than a day away from reaching us and it is spread out over two miles wide. They would never make it without being seen.

A few of the survivors decided to take the risk earlier today, while the rest of us decided to fortify our location in an attempt to keep the zombies from getting to us. We piled up rocks and destroyed the stairs as best we could. The closest ledge to us is at least 10 feet high now. There is virtually no way for them to get up to us individually; the only way up would be for them to make some sort of zombie pile where one would lay on top of another, so the zombie on top could reach us; I am really hoping they are not smart enough to figure that out. Unfortunately the rain has slowed us down so much. We also made one fatal mistake; we forgot to get extra zombie blood before we blocked everything off. We were able to find two dead zombies that had been blown up by the air strikes, but most of their blood had already been drained or dried up. I hope it is enough to keep us safe.

I can feel them getting closer. It feels like a small earthquake rumbling under us, even though they are still a mile or so away. I can only imagine the quaking that will take place once they are around us.

Ok, I have more preparations to make before they get here. Looks like another night without sleep.

Day 89

They are here.

The earth is shaking worse than I had thought it would and I am beginning to worry about the stability of the garage we are in. Early this morning we decided to hide in a few parked vehicles on the top floor. Everyone is in a separate vehicle except for Tonya and Cole. I am in an old Dodge Neon. God, I hope I don't die in a Neon!

The floor has been shaking and I can see a few of the barricades beginning to fall due to the "zombie quake". I don't know how much more the buildings can take. I also don't know how much more we can take. The loud moaning could be heard last night when they were still quite a distance away. Once they got here this morning, the noise was almost unbearable. They have been walking under us for a few hours now and I feel like I am going insane because of the moaning and groaning. I know the others are the same, because every now and then I peek out of the window and can see the others covering their ears. Alisha is rocking back and forth in her car right now and I can tell she looks panicked and stressed. I just hope we can all maintain for a little longer.

One other problem we are facing is the weather. Winter is quickly heading our way. I don't know what the temperature was this morning, but I know it was cold.

Sitting in a parked car in the frigged weather after being covered in cold zombie blood is not an easy thing to do during normal conditions. I know Shaughn has got to be cold, he is wearing shorts and a T shirt; at least the rest of us are in jeans.

Oh no! I can hear someone starting to cry. If I can hear it, I know those undead bastards can too. I have to go try to shut up whoever it is or we are all dead.

Day 90

The moaning is enough to drive anyone crazy, I guess. Imagine over a million people moaning at the same time over and over again. It is a constant "aaaaghhhhhhhwwwww". Only, it never seems to end. Words cannot describe accurately how the moaning actually feels on the body. To me, it feels like bugs crawling all over me. Every time there is a large group moan, my skin literally crawls; all the hair stands up on my arms and down my back. I just want it to stop. I would do anything to make it stop. I guess that's what Cheri was thinking also, when she began to cry yesterday. I tried to help her, I swear I did.

I tried to calm her down.

I tried to shut her up!

So I left the "safety" (if that's what you can call it) of the Neon, ran over to a nice brand new black Infinity, where I could see a girl crying. I convinced her to open the door to let me in. Once inside, I could clearly see that she was in a total panic. I asked her for her name and told her mine. She told me her name was Cheri then asked me to kill her. I was shocked! I asked her to calm down and think about what she had asked. She just kept saying that she couldn't take it anymore; the constant moaning. She said she could hear voices in the moans, voices calling out to her, telling her to join them. As she spoke, a cold shiver rose up my spine. Maybe that's why the moaning creeped me out so much, maybe it was voices I heard in the moans as well. Maybe that's why the girl ran out onto the streets in the city; maybe she heard the voices too. Hell, maybe I'm just going crazy...maybe we are all going crazy.

With out warning, she bolted out of the car, running as fast as she could towards the edge of the parking garage. I jumped out of the car and ran after her. Ed also jumped out of the truck he was hiding in. Cheri stood on the edge looking over at the undead crowed below her. She was sobbing uncontrollably. Ed quietly called out to her, begging her to step back from the ledge. She turned to look at us; she was no longer crying. "I'm sorry, they are telling me to" was all she said before turning back to face the crowed. Like an Olympic diver doing a perfect swan dive,

she spread out her arms and jumped into the masses below. I couldn't take a chance on going to the edge to look and see what had happened, but based on the sounds of the thud of her body crashing down to the ground, and the sounds of skin being ripped off of muscle, I can only imagine what the last few seconds of her life was like. I really hope the impact killed her before the zombies did.
Ed and I slowly walked back to our own vehicles. As he was walking away, he looked me directly in the eye and asked if I heard the voices too. "No" I told him.

I lied.

I do hear them. I hear what Cheri heard. Another black cloud is moving towards us.

Day 91

Rain again.

It's been raining all day again. I can't complain about it this time though, because the sounds of the drops on the hood of the car helps block out the moaning, plus it also helps wash away some of the stench in the air. I need something to block out the moaning and the voices. I swear I can hear them begging me to join them, to allow them to feast on me. I think I am going crazy. When I concentrate really hard, all I hear is moaning; it is when I stop concentrating that I can hear voices calling out to me. They are like quiet little whispers. I hope they will be gone soon. I cannot take much more. All night and so far all day today have been the constant rumbling of the feet below us, the moaning, and the sounds of rain.

How long have I been awake? Hell, when was the last time I even closed my eyes for more than two minutes? It sounds like they are moving away! The moaning has died down a little. Maybe I will be able to get some sleep tonight! The "calling out to me" has finished now, or maybe I have blocked it out of my head finally. I hope they will be gone tomorrow, so we can finally figure out what we are going to do. We cannot survive around here with those mass migrations coming and going. I think we all know things will never be the same, but maybe we can find somewhere to live out the rest of our lives where we won't have to be on the lookout every minute. First though, I have to try to find Darcy. One way or another, I have to know what happened to her. If we can leave this area tomorrow, we should be at the base as early as tomorrow night.

Day 92

I slept harder than I have ever slept my entire life. I had strange dreams. When I awoke, I was in my bed. Darcy was lying snuggled up against me like she had been for the past few years. I raised my head to look around.

Disoriented.

Where was I?

The sight of my bedroom took me aback. What the hell was going on?? I fell asleep and I was in a Neon, surrounded by zombies below me, now I was laying in my bed, in my room; all was well and as it should be. The zombies were a nightmare. I breathed in, the stench was gone. Darcy woke up and asked me if everything was alright. I smiled and said "yes, it is perfect". She ran her hands through my chest hairs and fell back asleep. I couldn't sleep, I was given a second chance at life.

I got out of bed and made a huge breakfast. I made eggs, grits, bacon, pancakes, and toast. When it was done, I took Darcy a tray in the bedroom for breakfast in bed. Together we ate it all. She kept commenting on how much I had changed overnight and even joked about aliens stealing the real me. We laughed a lot. Things were back to normal.

Without warning, the alarm went off. It was time to go to work. Aggh, at least during the zombie attack, I didn't have to go to work. I showered and got ready for the day. When I was leaving, I kissed Darcy like I hadn't done in years. Again with the alien comments.

Work was...well, work. I fixed computers and set up networks. I took a long lunch. I also got written up for something stupid I did weeks ago. I passed by one of the offices, a goldfish happily swam around in his bowl. People came and went. Things were normal again.

That night, Darcy and I sat around the house talking about wedding plans. I wanted to go to Vegas, she wanted to go to St. Lucia and get married on the beach. We argued a little about it, and then decided to pick a location in a few weeks. Darcy cooked her meatloaf that I love. We watched TV and went to bed early. We fell asleep a couple hours later. Things were normal again.

Days turned into weeks that turned into months. Life was normal. Life was good. I came and went to work; Darcy and I were planning our wedding, detail by detail. I still voted for Vegas. Every night I kissed Darcy like I hadn't seen her in years. I vowed to continue until the day I die. Life was normal again.

Last night I went to sleep like I had done every day before. I awoke this morning cold. The forgotten stench of death was in the air once again. I sat up quickly. Alisha and Ed were standing by the edge of the garage, looking at the area. Cole was talking to one of the other survivors, another teen; I think his name is Matthew. Jeremiah and Tonya were arguing with Shaughn. The sun was coming up. The zombie cloud was on the other side of the city. I got out of the car, walked to the edge, and took in the surroundings. Blood covered the ground. Bodies were torn to shreds and strung around on the ground. Buildings were crumbled and a straggling zombie or two picked clean the body of a young black girl. I blinked a few times and threw up. Things were normal again.

Day 93

As we began leaving the parking garage this morning, we heard a noise from inside a nearby dumpster. Jeremiah approached it cautiously, weapon in hand, and ready to blast apart anything that moved. He flung the lid wide open and shoved the barrel of the gun into the trash. Out of nowhere, a 2x4 smashed him across the nose, causing blood to fly in every direction. From out of the dumpster, holding the other end of the piece of wood was none other than "Mego". She flew out of the dumpster with ferocity, 2x4 pulled back, ready to strike again, until she saw who we were. She dropped the weapon and ran to help Jeremiah up. The rest of us followed. "Mego" was all too pleased to see the rest of us. Once our hellos were said, I told her our plan to head to the Military base to get any weapons, supplies, and survivors we can find. She agreed to go with us; after all, "the living must stick together to survive."

We have been walking all day and most of this evening. We have only encountered a few zombies, and most of them were completely immobile. There were a few that only had the upper portion of their bodies, so they were crawling around on the ground, pulling themselves along. The others, we disposed of as quickly as possible.

Now we are just outside the gates of the base. The gates have been torn down, and there are bodies everywhere. Hundreds or thousands of zombies, holes blown through their heads, laying along the ground, along with mutilated soldiers, every one of them have holes in their heads as well. There must have been one hell of a fight that took place here. We have decided to approach the base in the morning, so we can see a little better. I hope some people were able to escape. I hope Darcy was able to escape....if she was even there to begin with.

God help me, I feel terrible, but I don't care whether or not anyone else made it, I am being so selfish, but with everything I have been through, I think anyone would be selfish in a time like this.
Tomorrow can't come fast enough.

Day 94

The base is completely destroyed. Every building that once stood has been completely demolished. It looks as if someone hit a self destruct button, causing the entire base to explode. Pieces of rubble litter the ground, as do pieces of body parts. There are a few parts still moving. We saw a leg moving around on the ground, as were a few hands here and there. While sifting through a downed building, we found a decapitated head, with most of the face burned off, yet its eyes still followed us as we passed. Shaughn bent down to get a closer look at it, and almost got bit as it snapped its teeth at his face. Laughing, Cole and his new friend Matthew decided to play soccer with the head. Matthew was the one to score by kicking the head into the nearest tipped over trash can. Both of the teens jumped up and down, waving their arms around in victory.

Ed has been franticly searching for his family. There were three fallout shelters located throughout the city and we had found two of them. Both shelters were empty. They had been destroyed from the inside out, like someone set off bombs inside the shelter, killing everything and everyone inside. The doors to both shelters were off their hinges. Inside the lights were all destroyed, so it was too dark to really see what had happened, but the rooms were caked in blood. We would not let Ed in either of the shelters; we didn't think he could handle it, so we took a picture of his family and entered one at a time, searching for any signs of them. While searching, I also looked for signs of Darcy, though we found nothing that would lead us to think either of them had been in there. I don't know what happened in those shelters and I don't think I ever will, but whatever it was, by the looks of it, it was a living hell.

We have made our way to the last area of the base. We are directly outside the last shelter now. From what I can tell, the doors are still intact and closed tight. We are sitting outside, trying to figure out what to do. The shelter has a call box, where we can make contact with anyone on the inside, but no one is answering. We have thought about blowing open the doors, so we can get inside, but I don't think we have enough explosives to even do that, plus we don't want the kind of attention an explosion like that would make.

It's getting pretty late, so I think we will set up a camp for the evening. A few people will sleep, while the others look out, then we will swap, so we all can at least get a few hours of sleep. We are also going to continue to call the shelter; hopefully, someone is inside that can answer us...

The door to the shelter is opening slowly, as if someone is pushing it open, to peek out. I see someone's face...it's hard to make out, but I think it is a woman. It is a very pale face, looks to be covered in blood. Alisha is approaching cautiously...she has a flashlight. She is about to shine it on the girls face so we can see her......

It's Darcy.

<u>Day 95</u>

    Seeing Darcy last night for the first time in over three months was one of the happiest moments of my existence. Even covered in blood, she was as beautiful as the day I met her. I was completely in shock to see her, peering through the door. I was so happy; this is what I have dreamed of for so long. We were finally going to be together again. Things were going to be perfect.

    However...

    When Alisha approached her, she shined the light directly in Darcy's face. Once I saw it was her, I yelled for her and began running in that direction. Alisha turned to look at me; she was smiling at me, knowing how happy I would be. As I got closer, I saw Alisha turn back to face Darcy, it looked like she wanted to ask her a question or to say something to her. Before she got fully turned, Darcy jammed a butcher knife deep into Alisha's throat, pulled it out, and jammed it in again and again, over and over, until I got close enough to pry the knife out of her hand. Darcy looked directly at me. She had no idea who I was. She then shoved me out of the way and slammed the door shut, locking it and enclosing herself in the shelter again.

    I fell to the ground, grabbed Alisha and held her as she died in my arms. I told her it would be ok and that I was sorry for what happened. Thankfully, she died quickly without suffering too much. Everyone gathered around us, simultaneously felling sad and enraged at what had just happened. Jeremiah ran to the door and began screaming at Darcy. If he had the power, he would have ripped the door off its hinges right then and there. Cole and Matthew grabbed a hold of "Mego" with a death grip that no one would be able to pry open. Ed and Shaughn went to go calm Jeremiah down.

    I sat on the ground, wild thoughts racing through my head. I was covered in the blood of a friend...blood that my lover had drawn. What went through her head? What was she thinking? I know she saw me. Maybe she was scared and didn't know what was going on. I couldn't help but think about her on the other side of the door. As shocked as I was, my heart pounded more because she was near me and alive.

    We have to get inside.

    I have to know what is going on.

    I am scared for her life now though. Jeremiah wants

her dead. I am not sure about how the others feel. I will not allow anyone to hurt her. I will do whatever it takes to protect her...even if it means using the butcher knife myself.

Day 96

We buried Alisha in a shallow grave near the entrance to the shelter. Jeremiah stood at the door, staring at it as if he could kill Darcy through the door. He waited and I am sure prayed she would walk out that door, so he could end her life like she ended Alisha's. He paced back and forth, screaming at the door and every now and then he would turn and stare at me, as if I am the one that killed her. I felt like everyone blamed me. I have never felt so alone in all my life. Maybe it is my fault; after all, I had pushed everyone into following me to the base. Maybe I am responsible for Alisha's death.

After hours of the evil stares, Tonya went to talk to Jeremiah, to calm him down a little. I could not hear what they were saying at first, then as the conversation went on, Jeremiah's voice got louder and more belligerent. He turned and looked directly at me, pointed his finger towards me and yelled directly in Tonya's face "if that bitch doesn't come out here in the next few minutes, I will fucking kill that bastard who brought us here." At that, I jumped up and went over to him. I was not going to let anyone call Darcy a bitch, I don't care how big they are or in his case, how much military training he has. We got into a screaming match for a few minutes until "Mego" and Tonya split us up.

I can see there will be trouble, big trouble very soon. This kind of hostility can not last forever before it turns to violence.

Cole just yelled about a group of zombies heading our way.

I've got to go hide.

<u>Day 97</u>

The looks from the others have almost become unbearable. The only people still talking to me are Tonya and Cole. Jeremiah has convinced the others that Darcy killed everyone in the shelters, including Ed's family. I have no idea what to think. My guess is that she went crazy from all the moans and (I don' know what you would call them), maybe "subliminal" messages. All I know though is she is not herself in any way. Darcy is the kindest gentlest person I know and has never even been in a fight; until of course she stabbed Alicia to death. Maybe she just didn't recognize me. I haven't shaved in quite a while now and my hair is out of control. I have been trying to contact her through the call box, but have gotten no response. I am going to assume the box is broken.

Early this morning after the stares and shitty comments I have gotten from the other survivors, I told them all to just leave me alone. No one left though. I don't know if they are staying because they need leadership or if they want to see what will happen if Darcy comes out. I am not going to leave. If I have to stay here forever, I will not leave this place without Darcy. It has taken me this long to find her, I am not about to leave her, not now, not ever.

The zombie sightings have been very low today. Tonya told me she ran into a few earlier this morning while searching for some food, but nothing major. The ones from last night were taken out pretty quickly. With every bit of anger and frustration, Jeremiah took out three of them by himself with just a broken piece of fence post. Ed and I took out the other two. They remind me of roaches, as soon as you kill one or two, three or four more take their place.

I have been busy coming up with a plan on where to go once I get Darcy out of that shelter. There is mountain just on the outside of the city, just about 20 miles from here. The mountain sticks out like a sore thumb, because it is the tallest natural "structure" in the entire state. I remember Darcy and me walking up it a few years ago with my sister and nephews. There is only one easy way up that mountain, every other way is too steep to walk up and unless the undead bastards learn to climb a mountain, we can completely block off the path and we should be safe for a while. I remember there is a huge garden located on top of the mountain that we could use for growing vegetables and there is plenty of wild life around there for hunting. We could drink the rain water that we collect, so water would not be an issue. It's not the best plan, but it is all I can think of right now. The only major problem is lack of electricity. It will be like being back in the Middle Ages all over again.

Tonya and Cole have agreed to go up the mountain with Darcy and me.

Now all I have to do is get her out of that shelter and away from the others.

Day 98

Last night, while we were eating, we were surprised by a small group of zombies. I don't know how they got to us without being spotted. Maybe we were all preoccupied with our own thoughts. Jeremiah couldn't take his eyes off me. I now know the meaning of "if looks could kill". The others looked like they were confused about what to think. I had just opened my can of beans when Cole jumped up, and yelled "Oh crap, behind you!" I turned just in time to avoid having the back of my neck turned into someone (or some things) dinner. The zombie lunged for me as I stood up. He fell directly face down onto the ground. When he raised himself off the ground, his nose was turned sideways, now, clearly broken. As the zombie began getting to his feet, Cole's friend Matthew landed a nice blow to the back of its head with a brick. The blow didn't kill it, but it did knock it down long enough for "Mego" to drive a steel beam through his skull. Just as that one went down, three more were on us. Ed, Jeremiah and Shaughn were taking care of those three. As I went to assist, I was ambushed by another zombie. This zombie appeared to be running! I heard the foot steps before I saw him. That may be why I didn't think anything about it, because it was fast, much faster than any other zombie I had ever encountered. I guess I thought it was someone coming to help, maybe I wasn't thinking at all.

The zombie almost football tackled me he was running towards me so fast. By the time I saw him, he was already on me. As I fell back, he brought his mouth down towards my face. Instinctively I threw my hands up to block the bite. I caught him just under his jaw, successfully keeping him from chewing on me. While I was on the ground, I looked to the left to see if I could find a weapon, anything that may help me get him off me. I looked over long enough to see the shelter door swing open.

Darcy came running out, full speed towards my

location, carrying a sword! It was the type of sword that Marines carry on their dress blues. As she ran towards us, sword held up in the air, ready to deliver a powerful death stroke to the zombie, a single hand reached out from beside her, grabbing her by the hair, successfully yanking her off her feet and sprawling backwards. I could hear her grunt of anguish, pain, and frustration. She was screaming and crying.

Jeremiah was clearing the hair and scalp from his hand from where he grabbed Darcy. He pried the sword out of her hands. As she lay on the ground, facing up at the sky, Jeremiah filled her line of vision with his body. I could not tell what he was saying to her, I could just see the confusion on Darcy's face. I wanted to be there holding her, helping her through this. Jeremiah raised the sword over his head, ready to drive it through her body.

I was filled with rage! With a force that even scared me, I shoved the zombie off me and sent him flying into the air. My adrenalin was flowing as it has never done before. I saw red. I lowered my head and ran quickly towards them. My shoulder caught Jeremiah in his side, by the sounds of it I probably broke three or four ribs. He let out a cry as he hit the ground a few feet away. There I was, standing over Darcy. I could see her eyes, she could see mine. She recognized me, but only for an instant, before her eyes glassed over and to her, I was the enemy once again. It was as if I were staring at a stranger.

I picked up the sword and helped Darcy to her feet. I walked over to the zombie and with one quick swipe, I severed his head from his shoulders. Darcy grabbed onto me as if I were her savior. Together we made our way to a building just across the way from the shelter. I did not invite the others to join us, and also warned them not to attempt to harm Darcy in any way. I asked them to give me one night with her before they came to the building; I needed to try to calm her down.

After hours of crying and screaming, she finally fell asleep, where she has been the rest of the day. She still does not know who I am. She has, it seems, lost her mind completely. I just hope I can bring her back at some point. I have my Darcy back, for better or worse and nothing will separate us again.

A few of the others are heading this way with their bags. Jeremiah is not with them.

It looks like we will be heading for the mountain soon.

Day 99

Darcy slept most of today. When she was awake, she was completely unaware of her surroundings. She had no idea where she was or who I was. I tried to keep her calm as best I could, though I have to admit I was very thankful when she slept. I refused to leave her side. I know she will snap out of this, she has to. She is a very strong person.

While I was busy taking care of Darcy, "Mego", Cole, and a few of the others went to find supplies and weapons. While they were out, a few of the other survivors came in to check on Darcy and find out what the plan was. It seems as if everyone has either forgotten what she has done, or has forgiven her because of her mental state; everyone except Jeremiah.

From what the others have told me, Ed went through the shelter, looking for any signs of his family, but has found nothing that would indicate they were in there. It would appear as though they never made it to the shelters as he had thought. I pray that they made it to some safe place, but with the enormous size of the zombie cloud, it is not very likely.

As much as people kept asking, I refused to tell them the plan. I do not want to have to tell everyone individually what we are going to do, and I also don't want to have to argue with anyone about this. People can either go with me or stay here.

"Mego" and the others came back about an hour ago.

They brought quite a bit of canned food, lots of bottled water, enough weapons and ammo to arm a small country, and best of all, they brought it all in a huge military vehicle. The truck they brought looks like a personnel transporter, but it has plenty of room for everyone and our supplies.

With the truck already loaded, all I have left to do is hold a "survivor meeting", to fill everyone in at once and to map out our plan of action on getting there. We are not too far away from the mountain right now, in fact, you can see it from here. It is a strange sight to behold; a huge mountain made of nothing but rock, almost straight up on all sides except for one; that one side has a very narrow path leading almost straight up itself, but it is possible to hike up it, if you are fit enough. We have lots of planning to do. I am thinking we will leave in a few days. I want to give Darcy enough time to rest and relax before we confuse her even more.

Someone is yelling something outside. I cannot make out what they are saying though. It sounds like they are saying someone is coming. I think that is Jeremiah. "Mego" just screamed at something or someone.

It is Jeremiah.

He is covered in blood and being followed by a migration of zombies as far wide as I can see.

We are not waiting a few days, we are leaving NOW!

Day 100

Yesterday, after Jeremiah got to us, we threw everything and everyone into the truck and took off. Luckily we were able outrun the migration, though it was a little scary there for a while. Zombies were jumping towards the back of the truck as we drove off. Shaughn and Ed were in the back with the others, shooting zombies if they got close to us.

All the plans are set in motion. We will get to the mountain by the end of this evening. Once we get there, we are going to set up the explosives around the base of the path leading up the mountain. That should create a large enough barrier and trench that nothing will get past. Just in case something does get past, we are going to set up traps all along the way. We should be ok for quite a while up there, as long as we can keep from killing each other.

Jeremiah has not said anything to anyone since he got back with us. He has sat up front with Darcy and me and has been staring out the window. As for Darcy, the only sounds she makes are an occasional grunt in between hours of crying. She has been sitting beside me for some time now, rocking back and forth and waving her hands in front of her face, as if there were bugs flying around her. Probably the last hour or so, she has sat quietly with her hands in her lap just like she used to do when we would take our long drives to the beach.

We stopped briefly to get the last few supplies we needed before we get to the mountain at a large shopping center. Tonya and "Mego" took some of the other survivors to gather clothes for the winters and summers to come. The rest of us gathered supplies at the hardware store. We grabbed bags of seeds and quite a bit of lumber, pretty much everything we should need to last us a while.

As we were putting the last few items in the truck, Darcy turned, looked me directly in the eye and spoke to me. She actually acknowledged who I was! She asked me for a teddy bear to keep her company. At first I ignored it, thinking it was another wild rant she was on, until she grabbed my arm, and pulled me to her. She raised her hand, rubbed the now thick beard on my face, and said "Please baby, I need something to remind me of you once you are gone." It was Darcy again. She knew who I was...she may not have been all there, but she seemed as though she was getting better, more back to normal.

We were done gathering the supplies, we didn't need anything else, but how could I say no to Darcy, my love, besides it would only take a minute to run inside the store.

Without thinking, I ran as fast as I could to the toy store in the shopping complex. I ran to the stuffed animal section located in the back part of the store. Never had I ever been this excited about being in a toy store. Darcy was coming back to me and we were going to live happily ever after! I grabbed the best looking stuffed animal I could. The bear was dark brown with a cute smile plastered across his face and a hard red plastic nose. I held the bear up, to get a better look at it, in all its stuffed glory. This was the one!

    I was too excited,

    I got careless.

    I stuffed the bear under my arm and began running to the front of the store. Just before I got to the door, I was tackled by a woman; a zombie woman. There was nothing I could do except try to keep from getting my face ripped off. Her rotting teeth snapped down towards my neck. I moved under her in just enough time to avoid the bite. I could feel her nails as they shredded my shirt and skin. I tried pushing her off, but I was exhausted. Her next attack hit directly where she had aimed, ripping the skin and part of the muscle out of my forearm as if it were bread. My arm felt as though it were on fire. My blood splattered all over my face and began pouring onto the floor. I managed to get her off of me by rolling over onto my stomach and bucking her like a bronco. In the process, I was also bitten on my left shoulder. When she was off of me, I grabbed the closest thing I could find, the cash register. I raised it above my head and brought it down as hard as I could across her face. I continued to bash her with the register until there was nothing left of her head but a bloody mush.

I ran to the bathroom and washed and dressed my wounds as best I could. I had to stop the bleeding or I would be one of them before I got out of the store. After what seemed like hours, I had controlled the bleeding to a slow drip instead of a flowing river. Shaking, I went back to find the bear. He was covered in my blood and some brain matter from my attacker. I went back to the shelf to find the perfect bear again. Nothing seemed right. My head was swimming. I couldn't think straight. I grabbed the closest stuffed animal I could find and headed back towards the truck. As I passed my attackers' lifeless body, I could see a security badge hanging from her belt. I leaned down to pick it up. I had to know who she was. I had to know who dammed me and ended my life as I know it. The badge read "Stephanie".

As I approached the truck, everyone could see the state I was in. My shoulder bled through my shirt and blood ran down my hand from the bite on my forearm. "Mego" was the first one to me. She slowly pulled out her shotgun, yelled at me to stop and pointed the gun directly at my head. I closed my eyes. I could hear Tonya and Cole scream my name. I heard running. I fell to my knees, awaiting the blast that would end my life.

The shot never came.

As "Mego" was about to pull the trigger, Jeremiah stopped her. "He has a few more days left if we can stop the bleeding now". As I opened my eyes, Darcy came running over to where I was. She threw her arms around me and began to cry. Together we walked to the truck. All eyes were on us. I handed her the stuffed fox I had grabbed on my way out of the store. As I handed it to Darcy, she asked me what she should name it.

"Stephanie", I told her.

I gave no explanation and helped her back into the truck.

We should be at the mountain in about an hour. I have very little time left. I have to ensure the others are safe. I have to know that Darcy will be well taken care of. She is asleep with her head on my shoulder right now. I am going to miss this moment. I will miss our life.
I am going to try to enjoy the last few hours we have together.

Day 101: The end is just the beginning

This will be my last entry.
I can feel the infection riipping through my body, killings everything inside me as it takes over. Reality hasn't quite sunk in yet that in a few short minutes I will be deadd.

Last night when we got two the mountain, we imediately began setting up the explosives around the path. Thanks to the United States government, we had more than enough high powered exxplosives to blow up a small country. As we worked, Ed paced back and forth behind me, never taking his eyes off me; not that I blame him… Darcy was in and out of it all night. Half the time she would know who she was and what was going on, the other half she was completely unrresponsive.
Sometime early this morning, Tonya, who was our lookout, yelled to us that two very large migrations were heading our away. That new's made us work even harder and fasster. As the evening came to a end, I tried to spend much time with Darcy as I could while she was in her right mind. We talked about everything we could talk. I held her while she cried herself to sleep. We laughed a lot at the stupid things in the past now mean nothing. She was like someone with Alsheimers; one minute she was fine, then next she had no idea who I am.

By early this morning, all the preparation was complete. "Mego" took Cole and Mathew and a few of the other survivors up the mountain to prepare everything and to search for food and straggler zombies.

From were we stood, you could see the migration heading our way. Both groups had merged to form one huge cloud like shape coming straight towards us. At the rate they were moving, it was clear they would be on us by mid afternoon. My health was flailing fast. I guess all the work I been doing pumped the infection through my body faster. It was time to say goodby.

            Darcy stood beside me once again in her own little world. One by one, everyone walked by, giving me their condoollences. Noone was sure exactly what to say, after all, what do you say to a stranger who is diing? Tonya and Cole were the last two to say the goodbyes. Cole had come running down the mountain as fast as he could, just to be there whem I left. He stood beside me, face wet with sweats and tears. Tonya hugged me as hard as she could until I finally made her backoff. These people had been my family, my closests friends.
I love them.
 I could smell the blood rushing through their bodies. It smellled sweet. I begun feeling an urge to eat. My stomache, as upset as it was, felt as if it were on fire. This hunger burned threw every part of my body. I could barely stand up at this point. I ask Shaughn and Ed to carry me to an abandonned car parked at the edge of the explosives. As they begun to carrry me down, Darcy snaped to her self

again. She came running towards us. I don't know if she was completely aware of whats was going on, but I do know thatt she knew something bad was happening. She knew we wood not see each other again. She threw her arms around me and begin to cry. She was yelling "take me with you" over and over again. I tried my bests to hold her and comfert her, but I was tooo weak. I begged her to stop crying...I alwayys hated it when she crieddd. I askd Ed and Shaughn to put me down and leave us alon for one minite. I will not share every thing we spoke abot in our last few minuts to gether, but I told her how much I lovved her and how prod I was of her survivig this long. Last I told her about this jornal I have been writing for 101 days. I tol her were she can find a copy once I am gon.. I askdd her to pass this along to all the other survivrs so one day the world will know what happpened to me and our small group of peoples.

I caled the guys backover to finish carying me to the car. I kissed Darcy on the forhead and said my final goodbys as I was bing carried away.
Ed and Shaughn put me in the car, handd me a gun and the remote to the explosuves. I told them togather everyon and run as fast they could up the mountain and to nott turn a round. They shuld run if their lives depend on it, it does. The survivol of the humanrace dependon their survival. That takes me to where I am know.

I can barelyty type. My boddy ache. Myy soul hurts. It not easy nowing your life about to end. I am seting in a car filed with liqid nitregen and exxplosive. I cant help but laugh when I thinnk abotthe looks that wil cross those undead bastard face when I thro the switch and blow us all too hell. If I canwait til th last minute, I should be able to0 get rid of mo0re half of them with just this firssst explsion. Once thisone goe off, there are three more set to kickoff. The forc shuld be strong enugh to ripp--[a hug cratter in q side of the mountaiiinn, make it immaossible for any one to got up it.

My vission is getttting wors bye the second and itis geting harder and hard too breathe As I look outthe window,,,, itisas if everithing is hapning in slow mo0tion. Cole behind Tonya who on her knees crying and holding Darcy. Jeree3miah is yel;ling for ever6one to foll;ow him Ed pulling on Coles shirt, urggbing him to leve the blast zaone. The hav all began runmning up the mountai8n. As my head swimm,s I turn to face the mill9ons of zombis heding my way. A I turn back to see my6 friends on last time,.. I pause long enogh to see myself in the m5irror. I lo0k years older, I guess weall doi, but my onc chubby cheks are now sink in. I cun see the vens under my sjkin as they turn a drk purple color and s2well. My onnce browneyes hav near loast al;l they pigmint in them and are all most completly white4.

As I turn to0 look for my friends and loved ones. They are no were in site or at least I can't no 0longer see them I turn my head one lastttime as the sun is blottd out of the sky by

shadows.
The miration is here4.

They are bangghing on the cqar tryin t0o get inhere I cant longer feel my legds. he top of the car has crushed from the wait6 of them top of here. They are hands alll; around me rippin my shirt6 of. Blood is pooAring out of my nose and eys and ther is a loud r8nging in my eards. I hop I have the strengh left in my bo0dy t hit the buton. I ca smell;l the rott of their5 bbbbbbbbodies as they begin ripping art the car piece y piece to ge3t to me.

This is it
I cam going to finish this noo0w.
Im scvccared, bu I now the enm,d is jst the begiing.
Good Bye Darcy, I lov you and h0pe you li9ve forevr

Toall yo zombi bastasrds
 burn in
helllllllllllllllllllllllllllllllllllllllllllllllllllllllllllllllllllllllllllllll
lllllllllllllllllllllllllllllllllllllllllllllll

Made in the USA